DATE DUE

APR 26 2007	
JUN 27 2007	
OCT 13 2007	
NOV 01 2007	
JAN 05 2008	
FEB 09 2008	
MAR 16 2008	
MAY 30 2008	

Season of the Burning Souls

Season of the Burning Souls

Ken Hodgson

FIVE STAR

An imprint of Thomson Gale, a part of The Thomson Corporation

Detroit • New York • San Francisco • New Haven, Conn. • Waterville, Maine • London

Set in 11 pt. Plantin.

LIBRARY OF CONGRESS CATALOGING-IN-PUBLICATION DATA

Hodgson, Ken.
Season of the burning souls / Ken Hodgson. — 1st ed.
p. cm.
ISBN 1-59414-482-6 (alk. paper)
1. Combustion, Spontaneous human—Fiction. 2. New Mexico—Fiction. I. Title.
PS3558.O34346S43 2006
813'.6—dc22 2006012779

U.S. Hardcover:
ISBN 13: 978-1-59414-482-0
ISBN 10: 1-59414-482-6

First Edition. First Printing: October 2006.

Published in 2006 in conjunction with Tekno Books and Ed Gorman.

Printed in the United States of America on permanent paper
10 9 8 7 6 5 4 3 2 1

This book is for my partner in crime, my wife Rita.

ACKNOWLEDGMENTS

I wish to thank my agent, Russell Davis, along with John Helfers, Mary Smith and Deb Brod at Five Star for making it happen. Also special kudos to Ed Gorman, Loren D. Estleman and Tony Hillerman for being such great storytellers.

The people of Silver City, New Mexico, were especially helpful in helping me accurately place the setting of this book. As always, any screw-ups are totally mine.

Heav'n but the Vision of fulfill'd Desire.
And Hell the Shadow from a Soul on fire.
—Omar Khayyám, *Rubaiyat*

To everything there is a season,
and a time to every purpose under the Heaven . . .
—Ecclesiastes 3:1

Chapter One

The Prophet was the first to die by fire that strange and terrible summer of 1943.

To Sheriff Sam Sinrod the stench of burnt human flesh was nearly overpowering as he bent over to measure the smoking hole in front of the long ornate walnut bar that graced the back wall of Dub's Place Cocktail Lounge.

Breathing through his mouth, the sheriff moved the yardstick he had borrowed from the wide-eyed owner, Dub Taylor, around the opening, making mental notes of the dimensions. Before standing he shouted through the hole to Dr. Bryce Whitlock, the coroner of Grant County, New Mexico, who had gone down into the basement to check out the charred remains of the Prophet.

"What do you see down there, Doc?"

Whitlock gave a cough and shouted, "Well, aside from a boot with part of a foot still in it, I can gather up all of the remains with a dustpan and whisk broom."

"Beats anything I ever saw," Sam Sinrod said, standing and allowing himself to breath normally. He yelled once again into the smouldering hole. "Do you need me to come down and help?"

A hoarse voice replied from the depths. "No, everything that can be recovered will fit in an old dynamite box I found on a shelf by the remains. I'll take care of the matter and be up in a few minutes."

The sheriff stepped back a few feet, clucked his tongue and surveyed the motley crowd of scattered customers who had remained with their drinks. Dub's Place Cocktail Lounge was one of several Silver City bars in the old part of town that catered to retired folks and those down on their luck, offering nickel beer, cheap wine or Mexican whiskey along with a free lunch of bologna sandwiches or a bowl of pinto beans. More than a few whiled away their days here playing cards, cribbage or talking about the war, though Sam suspected some might check out the competition after this calamity.

"Tell me once again what happened," Sheriff Sinrod growled to no one in particular. "People don't just go and catch fire all by themselves."

"If you'd been here you wouldn't say that," Dub Taylor said as he reached across the bar to retrieve his yardstick. "Phil, the Prophet, just come in and started on his first beer of the morning when he got a strange red flush to his face, began gurgling like he couldn't catch his breath then caught on fire like a dry tumbleweed and burnt a hole right through my floor. It'll cost me a fair piece of change to fix it back up like it was."

Sam shook his head. "Okay, this man you call the Prophet must have come in drenched in gasoline and committed suicide. That's the only way something like this could happen. Tell me what you know about him."

Dub Taylor tucked the yardstick away and poured himself a healthy glass of whiskey. The bar owner was a burly fellow who sported a broken nose and cauliflower ears from his boxing days with a traveling carnival during the Great Depression. Dub's hair was silver these days and his waistline was gargantuan, but the man wasn't one to spook easily. Yet the old brawler's hands trembled after he chugged the whiskey and set the glass back down on the bar, a fact that the sheriff took note of.

"His real name was Phil Pegler," Dub Taylor said. "We only began calling him the Prophet after he lost his mind from getting bit by a tarantula that come in on a shipment of bananas over at Giem's Grocery." The bar owner refilled his glass and took another healthy swig. "You should remember that, it was all over the papers."

"Yeah," Sam nodded, "this was about three years ago, a few months before the Japs bombed Pearl Harbor, if I remember correctly. The paper said Pegler worked for the state road department and had a wife and kids."

"That's right, his family still lives in the same little house on forty acres a few miles out on the Lordsburg highway. Well sir, that spider that nailed him was one of them bad South American types, not one of the harmless variety like we have around here. Phil dang near died. I heard tell he had a terrible fever that burned out his brain. When he got better he quit his job with the state road department and commenced to talking with God. Then he wandered into the hills just south of town and set up housekeeping in a little cave. He refused to have anything to do with his family or much of anyone who don't want to listen to his prophecies."

"He became a troglodyte," Dr. Whitlock said with a cough as he came through the open door that led to the basement.

Dub Taylor shrugged his massive shoulders. "I don't know for sure what religion he was, never said. Phil was dead certain he'd become God's own prophet, however. He would come in, drink beer and eat what was likely his only meal of the day on money his wife doled out from his disability check. Then he would commence to augur the future. He never caused any trouble and was generally a sight more entertaining than listening to war news on the radio."

"Ol' Phil called this drought we're in square on." A skinny man sitting at a table playing solitaire wheezed. "But he wasn't worth a fart in a whirlwind when it came to divining winning cards. If he had been, folks would've given him more credence. Volcanos blowing up and covering the sun fifty years from now kinda loses something when you compare it to winning a few dollars at a game of poker being played in the here and now."

"This Phil Pegler had no enemies to anyone's knowledge?" Sam Sinrod asked firmly. "I keep saying people simply have to have a reason to go and burn up."

"Like I done told you," Dub Taylor said with a tone of exasperation, "everyone liked the Prophet. After that spider bit him the bubble on his level never fit between the lines again, but you could say that about a lot of my customers. Hell's bells, Sheriff, this *is* a bar."

On a barstool, Dr. Whitlock set an open wood dynamite box that was filled with a few inches of gray ashes along with a worn and charred boot. He lit up a Chesterfield. "I've gotten all of the remains that I could gather of this Prophet fellow." He rolled his gray eyes from one person to the next. "Did anyone of you notice anything out of the ordinary before this man caught fire?"

"We're all telling you the truth," Dub Taylor said. "Phil Pegler drank half of a glass of beer, mumbled something about the heat, then lit off like a friggin' Roman candle. The whole thing took only a minute or so before what was left of him had burned its way into the basement. That's when I called the law and fire department." He cocked an eye at the sheriff. "Speaking of the fire department, where the heck are they?"

Sam Sinrod said, "There's a grassfire south of town keeping them busy. I'll call the station when I get back and tell them not to bother coming over here." The sheriff glanced at the box of ashes. "I'm still inclined to think this had to be a suicide by gasoline."

"Nope, the Prophet was dry as the blasted weather when he

came in here," Dub said firmly. "And nobody smelled any gas, either. That stuff stinks, you know."

"Once we get the name and address of everyone here," Dr. Whitlock said turning to the sheriff, "I suggest I take the remains to the morgue and see if I can find anything in the way of evidence."

"Yeah," Sam Sinrod sighed. "I suppose there's not much more we can do here. One of the first things I'll have to do is notify the family and try to find out more about the victim."

"I'll tell you one thing," Dub Taylor said, bending over the bar to glower at a thin tendril of white smoke rising from the charred edge of the hole in floor.

"What's that?" the coroner asked.

"Phil Pegler sure was no great shakes at being a prophet. Any decent soothsayer worth his salt should have seen something like this coming and had the courtesy not to go and burn a hole in my floor."

Chapter Two

Sam Sinrod drove the nearly worn-out sheriff department's 1938 Ford Fordor slowly along highway 90 that wound south through the Burro Mountains to the flat desert town of Lordsburg. He was in no hurry, the windows were rolled down, gravel crunched beneath slick tires that he hoped would survive the drive without blowing out. With the war had come rationing of many things, especially rubber. He could not help but wonder how many more times the cruiser's tires could be patched before he would be forced to fill out a stack of government forms to get another set.

The sheriff had dropped off the coroner along with the dynamite box containing the Prophet's remains at the hospital, then stopped by his office where he had phoned the fire department and left word for Freeman Bates, the chief, not to bother responding to a reported fire at Dub's Place. From a telephone directory he had located the address of the small farm where Phil Pegler's family lived. Now, in the torrid heat of a New Mexico summer afternoon he was on his way to do what he considered the most distasteful task a lawman had to do; notifying a family of a loved one's death.

To the southeast, brown clouds of smoke billowed relentlessly toward a cloudless blue firmament. Sam took note of rustling leaves on sparse oak trees scattered among fields of dead grass and cactus. The rising heat waves caused the withering countryside to shimmer like a motion picture that was out of focus. If they didn't get some rain soon. . . . The sheriff breathed a sigh of relief when he confirmed a strong breeze coming from the west. The wildfire was being blown away from Silver City and its multitude of easily combustible frame buildings. At least his town had been spared, this time anyway.

He lit a cigar, tossed the match into the ashtray and thought back on how strange the weather had been this year. During the first three weeks of March a parching wind had blown east from out of Arizona, melting snow from the high, craggy Mogollon Mountains where it normally lay in thick drifts until the summer solstice. Many creeks that usually burbled cheerfully along had dried to mere trickles, or ceased flowing altogether. Windmills on farms and ranches were beginning to pump only a fraction of the life-giving water they had in the past. With frightening regularity, many of the shallower wells and springs away from streams had started going dry. The once twirling and flashing blades of Aeromotor windmills lay stilled in the hot wind, like fallen soldiers in a war against drought.

A few people, such as his chubby deputy, Burke Martin, asserted the strange weather was an omen, a portend of evil coming their way. Sam Sinrod had shrugged off such suggestions as groundless superstition. At least he had until today.

All too soon, Sam found himself turning into a dusty driveway at his destination. The sheriff placed his cigar into the ashtray for safekeeping then slowed the cruiser to a crawl while he surveyed the pallid gray plank wood shack that sat alone in a sea of dry grass on a treeless plateau. A skinny tire from a Model T dangling as a kid's swing from a frame of scavenged telephone poles was the sole sign of levity. Inside a fenced pen that likely once held a family milk cow, a dust devil swirled drab dirt and bits of rusty tin. All things considered, the dilapidated house reminded Sam of too many sad homes he had seen during the recent Great Depression. Even the faded laundry hanging on a swaybacked clothesline in the front yard fluttered in the parching wind like flags of surrender.

Sam took note of a DeSoto Airflow, an automobile he considered even uglier than this pathetic shack, parked the Ford in front of the house and sighed. Then he shut off the engine and climbed out to do what must be done. He tarried a moment to check for biting dogs, which were all too common in outlying places such as this. Aside from wind-whipped trash, nothing moved in the stifling afternoon heat.

The screen door squeaked open, revealing a slender woman wearing a print apron. She eyed the sheriff's cruiser and stepped from the shadows onto the stoop. "Come in, Sheriff," her voice strong, obviously accustomed to talking over the strident noise of an ever-present wind. "I assume you're here about my poor Phil."

Sam swallowed and walked closer. He had learned the woman's name was Amanda from Dr. Whitlock who had quickly consulted the hospital records resulting from her husband's spider bite. Amanda Pegler, however, took the sheriff aback by her beauty. Blond, curly hair framed an angelic face that had somehow withstood the trials of life in the desert without becoming leathery and wrinkled. "Mrs. Pegler, you're right, I am here to see you about your husband. I have bad news, I'm afraid."

"I haven't had any good news for so long, Sheriff, I wouldn't know how to handle it if it came." She motioned with a dainty hand, nails painted sunset pink. "Come in out of the sun, I have some lemonade in the icebox. And you can call me Amanda, please."

"Thank you, ma'am . . . Amanda." Sam's eyes took a moment to adjust from the outside glare. The small shack was far neater than what he had expected. The bare wood floor was swept clean. An ornate walnut buffet along the wall displayed a set of fine china. While the lady had but few furnishings, she was a person who obviously had pride.

Amanda extracted a sweaty pitcher from an oak chest cooler, poured two glasses full of lemonade and set them on a wood table draped with white cloth.

"Phil is dead, isn't he?" Amanda asked matter-of-factly over her shoulder as she replaced the pitcher into the icebox.

"Yes," Sam answered solemnly. He decided it would be kind to withhold any of the grisly details. "Your husband died at Dub's Place bar around noon today." After a long pause he added, "He passed away quickly . . . he didn't suffer."

Amanda Pegler stood and smoothed wrinkles from her cotton dress. "I apologize for not acting surprised, but to me, Phil has been dead for near onto three years, after being poisoned by that awful spider." She sighed. "The boys are at the neighbors. I'll tell them when they get home. Benny and Leon are their names. They're eight and twelve, you know."

Sam nodded even though he knew only that the couple had children. He took a swallow of the lemonade. It was cold, sweet, and quite good. "The coroner has his . . . remains. You don't need to worry about expenses, the county will take care of the burying."

"Thank you, Sheriff. Things have been plenty hard for us lately. My husband had a disability pension from the state but wouldn't sign his name to the checks. Mr. Rothman, at the bank, let me sign for him, so I could cash them. Bless his heart. I left thirty dollars every month with Dub Taylor. Phil would've starved to death if he hadn't gotten something to eat there. His mind was completely destroyed by venom and fever." A sob caught in her throat. "People made fun of him . . . called him a looney."

"It's over, Mrs. Pegler. It's all over, now."

"It was over three years ago. We're just getting around to the burying."

The sheriff finished the delicious lemonade. "There is a five-thousand-dollar life-insurance policy on all state employees that I'm sure you're aware of. This also applies to pensioners and those on disability. I'll get a copy of the death certificate from the courthouse and send it off to the insurance company for you."

"Thank you, Sheriff. I've been told about the policy. The boys and me, well, we are planning to use that money to leave Silver City. I don't know where we will go, but a long ways away from here, that's for certain." Amanda brushed a hand through her silky blond hair and stared out a window across the desert to distant swells of brown smoke. "A place where it's cool and green. A place where we all can try and forget."

"Yes ma'am, I understand," Sam said softly. He said his good-byes, climbed into the stifling hot cruiser, started the engine and was gone, a small dust devil chasing him to the Lordsburg highway.

On the rise of a low hill past Graveyard Draw, a red GMC pickup parked just off the highway with a flashing red light took Sam Sinrod's attention. Two men, one of whom he recognized as Fire Chief Freeman Bates, stood waving their arms to flag him down for some reason.

The sheriff slowed before pulling off the highway to keep the following cloud of dust to a minimum. After the air cleared, he climbed out to see what the firemen wanted. He assumed it was about the call to Dub's Place.

"Glad to see you coming by, Sheriff," Freeman said. He was a tall older man, lanky and clean shaven. Freeman had been fire chief of Silver City for over twenty years. A competent, hard-working man, he was universally liked. "You saved us a trip to town to fetch you. We've found the darndest thing that started this wildfire."

"You don't know about the call to go to Dub Taylor's bar?" Sam asked.

Freeman squinted and shook his head. "Nope, this is the first I've heard of it. Dammit all, is his joint on fire too?"

Sam said, "There was an . . . ah, *incident* there earlier, but I left word at the station for you to cancel the alarm. The fire's out and the situation is taken care of."

Bates snorted, "I sure as hell wish we could get some of those modern two-way radios in our cars out here like they have in New York and other big cities." Then he thought for a moment. "I reckon they will never work out here in these mountains, blast it all anyway. It would be mighty nice to know what's going on before all that's left to squirt water on is a foundation."

"What have you got to show me?" Sam was anxious to get back to his office. He wanted to have some answers before being bombarded with the inevitable barrage of questions that would surely come.

"Follow us," Bates said flatly. "This is one of those things a person needs to see to believe." He and the other man climbed into the GMC and headed down a dirt road. In less than a half mile, they stopped where a long, north-south line of charring marked where the fire had started.

Sam Sinrod got out of his cruiser, wiped a bead of sweat from his right eye and went to see what it was on the ground the firemen had found interesting enough to stare at.

Instantly, the sheriff stiffened. On a flat patch of earth sheltered from the wind, exactly on the boundary that designated the beginning of where the grassfire had been ignited, were a still-smoking pair of work boots. Extending into the charred zone was the unmistakable outline of a human being defined by a thick layer of gray ashes.

"You ever seen anything like this before?" Bates asked the sheriff.

"I find it hard to believe," Sam Sinrod said, his voice dry as the earth on which he stood, "but I sure as hell have."

Chapter Three

Barth Thornton stood beside the cold steel autopsy table in the basement morgue of the Grant County Hospital. In the early days of Silver City, before refrigeration, miners had blasted an excavation deep into the cool granite mountain to use as a storage for such necessities as milk, meat and beer. Later, it had been enlarged and the hospital had been built above, allowing the chilly rooms to be turned into a morgue as a thrifty way to save on electricity.

Wearing a quizzical expression on his parchment face, he picked up and studied the boot containing a charred foot. A tall man with a skinny frame, Barth had been an undertaker in Silver City for over forty years. Nothing he had encountered in all of his long experience of caring for the dead, however, would allow him to give a sure answer to any of Dr. Whitlock's myriad questions.

"Why wasn't this foot consumed with the rest of the body?" the coroner asked, wafting a puff of smoke from his Chesterfield cigarette into the crisp air.

The undertaker took off his black horn-rimmed glasses, blew an annoying speck of dust from one of the lenses, then replaced the boot into the box of ashes. "What I would really like to know is how so much heat came to be generated in what you describe as mere moments. When I do a cremation, I have to run the oil burner at full blast for over two hours at a temperature of around eighteen hundred degrees to incinerate the deceased. Few people know that even after the cremation process, we're forced to use a grinder to pulverize various pieces of bone and teeth that are left on the floor of the furnace. Relatives can be quite fussy about the quality of the cremains."

"Cremains?" Whitlock said raising an eyebrow. "I have not heard that word before."

"That is the term we in the funeral-director business prefer to describe the remains of a loved one instead of ashes."

"That must help," Dr. Whitlock grinned and ran a hand through his coal-black hair that he kept slicked black with Wildroot Cream Oil. "People just keep dying to do business with you."

Barth gave a low groan, wishing he had a dollar for every time someone had said that to him. The coroner had spent too much time around Sam Sinrod, Barth decided. The young sheriff was well noted for spouting off an occasional wisecrack. Both men were simply young and undisciplined; Sinrod and Whitlock were only in their early thirties. At least they were conscientious and capable.

Barth gave a thin undertaker's smile. "And people *should* trust me. I am the last person on earth to let them down." His smile melted. "Now that we have exhausted some of the pedestrian jests those in my profession must endure, shall we proceed with the business at hand?"

The coroner snuffed out his cigarette. "How about we use a foot instead. I'm puzzled as to why it was not burned to ashes along with the rest of the body."

The undertaker replaced his glasses, his expression serious as he said, "All I can say for certain is that in my long experience with cremation and crematoriums, it would take hours to reduce a human being to the contents you have in that dynamite box. I can't figure the foot surviving except to wonder if possibly the boot choked off the supply of oxygen and stifled the combustion process. I honestly don't know."

Dr. Whitlock tapped a fresh Chesterfield from a pack, his face tight with concern. "I feel the same way, but if I put 'I don't know' on his death certificate, I don't think it would look good on my record come the next election."

Barth gave a knowing nod. "I can see your point, Doc. Perhaps it would be best for all concerned if we were to only refer to Mr. Pegler's rather odd fiery demise as being caused by an unknown but quite powerful incendiary agent, the nature of which is being diligently investigated."

"I'm inclined to agree with you." Dr. Whitlock stood to escort the undertaker to the door. He felt an onslaught of dizziness and was forced to lean on the steel autopsy table for support. "Thanks for taking the time to come by, Barth, I appreciate it."

"Under the circumstances," the mortician gave a nervous cough before continuing, "uh . . . I assume the county will want you to withhold burial for a while?"

"Yes, I'll have to, for a while, anyway." Weakness was coming in waves now. Dr. Whitlock knew the undertaker was fishing for the seventy-five-dollar fee he would receive from the county to handle Phil Pegler's burial, even though in this particular case a posthole digger would take care of the job in minutes. "But I can go ahead and put through the payment voucher. I'll talk to the mayor if a problem arises."

"Thanks, Doc," Barth said on his way out. "I appreciate you doing that, money is tight plenty these days, with the war and all."

Alone now, Bryce Whitlock grabbed a chocolate bar from his shirt pocket, tore away the wrapper and wolfed it down with two bites. Slowly, the feeling of weakness began to ebb. The diabetes that had kept him from the military service he so terribly wished for was controllable, but something he needed to hide. More than anything, the doctor had wanted to join the Air

Corps and become a flight surgeon.

The dapper airmen portrayed in movies were always getting the prettiest girls. It was the worst disappointment in his life when he could not pass the basic induction physical. Not even his friend Sam Sinrod knew of his malady. Civilian jobs not related to fighting the war were hard to come by. And elected positions were never filled by the imperfect.

Dr. Whitlock walked to the chair at the desk and slumped into it. He was glad his office was in the cool basement, the summer heat was stifling to him. After a few moments he pulled a Charles Dickens novel, *Bleak House,* from his desk. The coroner loved to read and the day had been a trying one, he deserved a break. This book was certainly not one of the author's best, but a real improvement after struggling through Herman Melville's plodding and nearly incomprehensible novel, *Moby Dick.* He flipped open the book to the cigarette paper he used as a marker, leaned back in his chair and began to read.

A few minutes later Whitlock's eyes grew wide. "Well I'll be a monkey's uncle," he said in utter astonishment.

Chapter Four

Payatt Hae's spring was dying. With a long-handled shovel, the wiry old Apache dug at the moss- and lichen-shrouded hole at the base of a red sandstone cliff. Hordes of bees and yellow jacket wasps, crazed for moisture, attacked the few heaps of muddy earth that had rewarded Hae's efforts to regain even a small trickle of the once plentiful water *Usen* had provided as far back as Hae could remember.

It was to no avail. Payatt leaned the shovel against a small cottonwood tree with withering leaves and stepped back to stare sadly at the now-barren spring. For some reason he could not comprehend, Payatt must have offended a god. That could be the only answer to such a predicament. But until the angered god was pacified there was only one thing he could do. He would be forced to buy water from the town of Silver City and haul it in a tank on the back of his pickup truck to keep his cattle alive and supply water for his home.

Payatt's rheumy eyes looked into the distance, across the fence that separated his property from the government's, to a shining windmill that stood tall at the base of Pictured Rocks. This was what had angered the god and was the cause of his spring dying. A *Pinda-lik-o-yi,* as his ancestors called the white-eyes, had just drilled a deep well and put up this abominable metal contraption that sucked life from the earth and dried the spring that had flowed since *Usen* himself had walked upon the earth.

Yet, there was nothing to be done. At least not anything the white man understood. The law would put him in jail if he destroyed that windmill, but he had a plan. Payatt would haul his water. But he would also dance another *Gahe.* He would put on his headdress of feathers from the eagle, amulets of turquoise from the Earth God. Then, alone and bathed in moonlight, he would sing chants and dance a *Gahe* to ask for help from the Great *Usen* to rid the sacred mountain of this windmill that was killing the life of his people. No matter which god was upset with him, *Usen* would intercede and make the deity leave his spring alone and restore the flow of water.

Payatt Hae had danced a *Gahe* for the safety of his grandson, Frank, who had joined the Army and had gone to some place called "South Pacific." His grandson had been there for a year and no harm had come to him. Perhaps, Hae thought hopefully, the *Gahe* to remove the windmill would be as successful.

Just two days ago, Payatt Hae had seen an omen in the night sky that gave him hope. A simple prayer, without dancing or beseeching the help of any minor gods, had sent a fireball flying toward the cursed windmill, thrown from Heaven by the mighty hand of *Usen.* The flaming ball had roared from a starry sky to crash into the earth just above the windmill.

"It was too bad that it did not strike it," Payatt said aloud so any spirits who were listening would hear him and possibly help. "The eagle feathers were what was needed. An eagle does not miss when it strikes a rabbit or snake. When I do the *Gahe,* the sharp eyes of an eagle shall surely guide *Usen*'s next fireball. It would be a shame for the Great God to miss that windmill again."

Steeled with determination, Payatt Hae picked up the shovel and began the short walk to his home. His shoulders and back ached and throbbed from the digging he had done. He was becoming old. Soon it would be time from him to join his ancestors in the World of the Great Spirit the Apache called *Usen.* This was as it should be. The pain was telling him to ready himself for the journey.

Payatt Hae stopped, turned and stared through the rising heat waves at the distant twirling blades of the hated windmill. In his mind's eye he could picture the smoking ruins that would soon be all that was left of the *Pinda-lik-o-yi*'s infernal machine. Then his spring would once again flow water.

Happier now, Payatt continued his trek. Chepi, his wife of many summers, was surely making fresh corn tortillas. He was hungry and it would be good to be home and out of the parching sun.

All gods, Payatt thought as he shuffled along, could be problems on occasions. The white-eyes claimed to have only one God. That would be even more difficult than having several to contend with. Many times the minor gods fought among themselves and forgot about The People. This was good. A single God, who was everywhere all the time, would certainly meddle too much with people's lives for comfort.

No, it was far better to have a small god dry up a spring than be a white-eyes and have to put up with one God and all of the problems that would entail. He caught the wonderful aroma of frying tortillas and hurried on to be where it was cool. Then he could rest and forget for a while about the work and expense of having to haul water.

Chapter Five

Wesley Clinkenbeard reached down, grabbed onto a handle of the steel-wheeled barrow and steadied it before their battered old wheelbarrow along with its strange cargo rolled off the trail and tumbled down the steep, rocky mountainside.

"Be careful, you old noodlehead," Wesley grumbled to Tasker Adams, who had been his mining partner for over forty years. "Watch it, that blasted thing, whatever it is, weighs more than a lead anvil."

"Ain't my fault you old codger, there's rocks on the trail and you ain't the one doing all of the pushing. Besides that, an egg would be easier to put a hook on than whatever this is we found."

"You know," Wesley said, "it would be a windfall for us if it turned out to be full of quicksilver." He took his hand from the wheelbarrow and began tamping the tobacco in his pipe before the fire went out. With the war going badly and rationing in effect, it would be an unnecessary waste to use a match if he didn't have to. "That quicksilver stuff would pay a lot more than scrap iron, I'm betting."

Tasker gave a grunt as he pushed his burden over a steep hump. "It's just too bad it didn't turn out to be a meteor like we'd thought it would be. Now one of those things might put us on easy street for quite a spell."

"That's a for sure. After we heard about that article in *National Geographic* where a meteor crashed through a barn roof somewheres up in North Dakota. A thousand dollars that farmer sold it for, to some museum. We could use a big piece of change like that, the way things are heading for Hades."

"Well, don't forget, that meteor did kill a good Guernsey milk cow along with a shoat pig and burn down the barn. All those costs need to be factored in. That farmer didn't make a big profit on selling his sky rock."

"Ours would have been all gravy, you old coot." Wesley frowned when he couldn't feel any fire left in his pipe. "All this thing did was singe a patch of worthless desert. It even missed that new windmill above old Payatt Hae's place."

"Been nice if that piece of round iron, whatever the hell it is, had landed on a shoat pig. We could use the meat. Pinto beans seasoned with chili peppers and only a taste of fatback is getting mighty tiresome, I'm here to tell you."

Tasker Adams took a moment to shake his head in a futile attempt to get a pesky blowfly out of his ear before continuing. "Well, the dang thing sure *looked* like a meteor, the way it came streaking in, shooting fire out of its tail like it did."

"I'm betting the thing fell off an airplane. Been lots of them flying around here of late for some reason. There's that new Air Corps base in Alamogordo. And I hear tell the government's doing a lot of secret stuff up near Los Alamos."

Tasker set the barrow on its pegs, swatted the blowfly from his ear and adjusted the eyepatch he had worn since that time in Colorado when he and Wesley were sinking a shaft on a gold mine near Central City. Tasker had looked up from the bottom of the shaft to see where the bucket was only to have a falling rock smash out his right eye.

"You don't think this thing we're hauling home is some kind of newfangled bomb do you?" Tasker asked worriedly. "We don't need that kind of grief."

"Nah," Wesley said with a dismissive snort. "If falling out of the sky and smacking into the ground hard enough to make a crater didn't set it off, I can't see where we need to fret any."

"Reckon you're right, pard, but I'm afraid all we're gonna likely get out of all this hard work in the summer heat will be a hundred or so pounds of scrap iron to sell. I'm of the notion that when we open it, there won't be any quicksilver. There's already a crack in one side that's only leaking out some thick green mixture that looks like grasshopper juice."

"It's just grease, to my way of thinking. Most likely it's water-pump grease, that stuff's green and thick, sort of like that."

"I can't see why the Army would fill a heavy egg-shaped cylinder with water-pump grease."

"Maybe they were making a grease bomb." Wesley frowned when he realized the fire had gone out of his pipe and he would have to wait until they got home to obtain a match. "Drop a bunch of grease bombs on the road and it'd make it slick enough the enemy trucks would slide off."

"And you call me a noodlehead." Tasker grabbed up the wheelbarrow. He couldn't expect his partner to be a lot of help these days. Wesley had broken his back a couple of years ago when he had fallen out of a bee tree they were trying to rob of honey. "Even the Army ain't that dumb. If they can get close enough to blow them up, why just cause them to get stuck? I swear, Wesley, if it weren't for me doing enough thinking for the both of us, we'd have starved to death long ago."

Wesley took a deep breath and decided to let his partner's tirade pass. Hot weather always did make Tasker irritable. "You have a good point, I'm now of the opinion it isn't a grease bomb. But there sure ain't no question about it being military, being painted olive green like it is and having numbers scribbled all over it."

"The fact that it has UNITED STATES ARMY written on it is a mighty good clue you're onto something. However, it was obviously abandoned. If we had just left it laying there, some thief would have come along and stolen it. The term 'finders keepers, losers weepers' applies to the military same as others, in my book."

"I ain't arguing with you none there," Wesley said as his partner pushed the wheelbarrow to a stop behind their battered Model A Ford pickup. "We're just being patriotic and helping out with the war effort. The government is begging for scrap iron and such. All we're doing is rounding up all that we can and selling it to them at a mighty fair price so we can afford to keep rounding up more. A few cold beers along with some groceries is only our just dues for all of our hard work."

"Yep," Tasker said as he dropped the tailgate and pulled out a couple of long wood planks to roll their prize from the wheelbarrow up into the pickup bed. "Fair's fair, and the government's got lots of money and we ain't, which makes it even more fair. Now do the best you can to help me get this blame thing loaded without straining your back so we can head home. It ain't getting any cooler out here you know."

A few moments later, the old Model A chugged onto the main highway and headed for Silver City beneath a blazing New Mexico sun. From the bed of the truck an occasional drop of green fluid splashed onto the dry, hot gravel where it instantly evaporated into the torrid breeze.

Chapter Six

Tasker Adams ground the gears on the nearly worn-out Model A truck as he attempted to shift into reverse and back it up a slight incline to the garage.

"You *are* a noodlehead," Wesley Clinkenbeard grumbled from beside him. "This is the only truck we have to drive. If you go and tear the gearbox out, that wheelbarrow's all we'll have to haul groceries in. And we won't even be able to do that because we'll be too broke to buy any in the first place."

"Be quiet you old codger," Tasker said, sticking his head out the window while backing up. "The clutch is plumb gone out. You know that. I swear you'd complain if you were being hung with a brand-new rope."

"We shouldn't have dropped by Dub's bar and then stayed so long. You always get testy after a few beers."

Tasker got the Model A as close to the garage as he could and still swing open the doors. It was only prudent to keep any prying eyes from surveying the contents. Quite a number of people might recognize something inside, then claim it was very similar to an item they had mislaid and cause them problems. He shut off the engine while Wesley jumped out to put chocks under the wheels to keep the truck from rolling away if the gearshift got bumped into neutral by accident. The parking brake hadn't worked for over a dozen years.

"There's nothing like a good cold beer on a hot day," Tasker said climbing out. "And don't forget that Dub always has free bologna sandwiches or something to eat. Things like that saves us money. Downright economical is what I'd call it."

"Twenty-two glasses of beer between the two of us at a nickel a toss adds up to a dollar. Ellie's joint sells mighty good hamburgers for a dime. And you call going to Dub's bar economical? I rest my case about you being a noodlehead."

"At least I can cipher. We spent a dollar and ten cents at Dub's Place, and I claim it was worth every penny. And Ellie don't serve beer."

Wesley Clinkenbeard's stubble-bearded face grew serious. "What do you make of that Prophet fellow coming in and catching on fire like he done? That was one big hole he burnt through Dub's floor. Lucky we have a few oak planks to sell him that'll match just perfect."

"They should match. When Otis Martin built Dub's bar, he used what was left over on that cabin of his up at Pinos Altos."

"Don't fret it any. Otis is in the Army somewhere in Europe. He won't be missing that floor for a long while."

"Yep," Tasker said, "and we're being downright generous by only charging Dub five dollars to fix his floor up like new. I'd venture the Prophet went and done us a favor."

"I still can't figure someone just plain burning up for no good reason. Downright spooky is what I say it is."

"Well don't strain your brain over the matter. Now, this military thing we've got covered up with a tarp, we need to get it inside so we can pry it open and see if we got more than plain scrap iron."

Both of the skinny old men turned to stare down the canyon of Little Walnut Creek to the uncomfortably close house that belonged to Sheriff Sam Sinrod.

They had filed a mining claim on a vein of copper that turned out to be worthless, but before its value had become obvious, the men had built a comfortable frame cabin along with a big garage. Then the sheriff had bought the nearest house soon after Wesley's accident with the bee tree, so they were stuck living close to the law.

It was difficult enough making a living hauling in scrap iron to sell, without the added problems of having the sheriff as their nearest, and only, neighbor. The saving grace was the fact that Sam Sinrod was young enough to be gone most of the time, which was an agreeable trait.

Tasker and Wesley had become quite proficient at their pilfering. Sweeney White's lawnmower had disappeared from his lawn while he was using it. The mailman had only stepped inside for a drink of water to come out and find it missing. Frank Armbruster was still wondering what had happened to the brass weathervane that used to be atop his barn.

Anything left at an abandoned mine was fair game. The old men judged being abandoned by the fact that no armed guards happened to be present at the time. Much of the mining machinery was too heavy to be loaded all at once, so they were forced to take only a few hundred pounds of smaller items at one trip. However, the pounds added up. Over the period of a year the old miners managed to sell Lonnie Dillman, the local scrap buyer, upwards of one hundred tons of "appropriated" material. Strictly to support the war effort, of course.

"Well," Wesley said after a long while, "the sheriff ain't about, so let's get this thing unloaded and under cover."

"Grab the planks and lay 'em out while I open the garage doors," Tasker said while turning. "It would be bad news if the sheriff decided to come home just when we have something in a position where we can't rush the proceedings."

A few moments later the damaged olive-green cylinder had been rolled into the garage and then slid alongside a duplex Gardner-Denver steam-powered water pump they had liberated from the High Lonesome Mine, then deemed it operable and too good to sell for scrap iron.

"I'm getting too pooped to do any more work today," Wesley said, forcing himself to stand with obvious pain. "Whatever is inside that thing will still be there tomorrow."

"Or the next day," Tasker added. "Remember all those cases of dynamite we found in that mine tunnel in Pinos Altos. We'd best get to hauling them in before someone less deserving comes across 'em. I'll bet we can sell that powder for five bucks a box and there's a good ten cases up there."

"You sure that dynamite ain't gone bad? When it does, pure nitroglycerine leaks out and makes the stuff mighty testy to handle. I saw some white crystals on some of those cases, and it wasn't frost."

"Wesley," Tasker fumed as they walked from the garage and closed the doors behind them, "if you didn't have me to kick the lead outta your lazy butt, we would never get by in this world. You worry too much, plain and simple. Bad dynamite isn't gonna blow up without good reason and we sure as hell ain't gonna give it one. We'll let whoever buys it from us do the fretting when they tamp it in a drill hole."

"Yeah, pard, you're right. We'll let the military thing wait for a while before we take a chisel to it." Wesley slung his right hand up and down. "I think it's full of some kind of acid, not grease."

"Why do you say that?"

"I got some of the green juice that's leaking out of it on my hand when we unloaded the thing. Now it's beginning to burn like it's on fire."

"Well, let's get inside the house. Wash your hands and I'll see if we have any baking soda, that'll stop an acid burn."

"Yeah, I'm right behind you. Dang, this *hurts.*"

"You always were one to complain," Tasker said. "It ain't

nothing to fret over."

"It ain't *your* hand," Wesley said, but a moment later, he felt just fine.

"Dag nab it," Tasker grumbled, poking through the kitchen cabinet. "I think you took up all of our baking soda the time I cooked up those habanero peppers and eggs. If we have any, I can't find it."

"My hand quit hurting." Wesley stared at his left hand as if he had never seen it before. "My palm felt red-hot, like it was on fire, then it just plain quit. The thing don't even look singed. I never seen the like."

"Then you ain't got nothing to complain about." Tasker shut the cabinet door. "Which is good, because your flimsy tummy couldn't handle good Mexican cooking and you went and used up all the soda for no good reason."

"Well, I'm gonna wash my hands just to be on the safe side," Wesley said, pumping the handle over the sink. "And for your information those blasted peppers were hot enough to burn the lint out of the Devil's belly button. That's likely why the Prophet burnt through Dub's floor, he ate some of your Mexican cooking."

"Simmer down, you old coot. We already had our dinner, so you don't have nothing to fret from any stew pot tonight."

"Yeah," Wesley Clinkenbeard studied his hand, wondering as to why it did not appear at least reddened after all of the pain. "Tomorrow's what concerns me."

Tasker ignored his friend. He turned on a hot plate to boil some coffee. The old miner was forced to wait to pump water to fill the metal porcelain pot, until Wesley had finally quit fussing with washing his hands. In over forty years he had never seen anyone scrub so hard at something that could not be seen. His partner was becoming a Caspar Milquetoast. Tasker sighed at the thought and hoped Wesley might get better when the weather cooled down. A summer hot and dry as this one had been was enough to drive anyone batty.

Chapter Seven

A lowering sun was blazing red over the Big Burro Mountains of southwest New Mexico when an exhausted Sam Sinrod drove into Silver City. His thoughts were in a quandary as to how to handle the incredible events of the day.

At the scene where the grassfire apparently started, he had used his Kodak camera to photograph the outline of the body. Then he and Fire Chief Freeman Bates had brushed what ashes they could recover into a cardboard box which, along with the pair of charred boots with feet still inside, were stashed in the trunk of the cruiser.

Only a few yards away from the body, to the west in an unburned area, he had found a .410 Stevens double-barreled shotgun, leaving him to believe the hapless person who had ignited the brushfire had been hunting, most likely for rabbits, which were plentiful this time of year. The sheriff postulated the hunter had dropped the shotgun after becoming struck by some malady, staggered a short distance downhill, then for some totally unexplained reason had burst into flames and set fire to the bone-dry grass.

"People aren't supposed to do that," Freeman Bates had said firmly, as if he expected Sam to arrest the remains.

But Sheriff Sinrod had no one to toss into jail. He didn't even have a clue what to write down in a report. To further complicate matters, Henry Fossett, the muckraking new editor who had just taken over as head of the *Silver City Times* would certainly blow the matter totally out of proportion and cause him grief. For some reason, Fossett actually seemed to relish blowing everything out of proportion, unlike good old Vernon Fisher, who had retired.

Perhaps, Sam thought, *this would be a good time to move to Montana and become a shoe salesman.*

Then he found himself pulling into a parking space behind the hospital. Sam noticed Thornton's somber black Cadillac funeral hearse turning onto the street, heading west, and wondered if a patient had passed away. He clucked his tongue and felt a pang of guilt for hoping any death had come by easily explainable causes. Gunshot wounds, knifings, car wrecks or obvious suicides were not all that difficult to handle. But two people bursting into flames for no discernable reason were pure pain for a lawman to deal with. There were laws and rules dealing with most every conceivable way a person could wind up dead. Bursting into flames for no good reason wasn't among them.

He cheered himself by hoping that possibly Dr. Whitlock had found both a cause and cure for the rash of incinerations that were beginning to plague his jurisdiction.

Sam's pencil-thin moustache formed a slight smile of relief as he climbed from the sheriff's cruiser, grabbed the brown cardboard box that, ironically, had once contained a dozen Fugo fire extinguishers. He tucked it under his left arm and headed down the ramp that led to the morgue.

"Dr. Whitlock is in his office," Tina Ortega said sweetly to Sam Sinrod. Tina was the coroner's newest nurse, a sable-haired young lady of twenty-five with a delightful figure who was as competent as she was lovely. She also had the good sense to have moved her office into a room across the hall from the morgue. This allowed her to avoid contending with the numerous grisly distractions that had caused Dr. Whitlock to suffer a succession of helpers.

"I noticed Barth Thornton's hearse leaving when I pulled in," Sam said, tarrying to spend a few moments with the lovely lady before going into the gruesome business of another totally fried corpse. "Did someone pass away here in the hospital?"

"No," Tina said with a bat of green-painted eyelids. "The doctor asked me to call Mr. Thornton in for a consultation about the man who caught on fire in Dub's Place today. That was such a strange thing for a person to do—catch on fire all by themselves. I am sure nothing like that will ever happen again."

The sheriff gave a dismissive shrug, turned slightly to keep the nurse from glimpsing the contents of the box under his arm and headed into the morgue. "I really wish you were right," he said. Before the nurse could question him further, Sam was closing the door behind him.

The coroner sat leaning back in his swivel rocker, legs propped up on the desk, smoking a cigarette and reading a book. "Hello Sam," Dr. Whitlock said without looking away from his book. "Grab a cup of java and take a chair."

Sam Sinrod sat the box on an examination table by the wall, poured a cup of what he expected to be excellent coffee, adding a spoon of sugar. He opined that in the history of hospitals and morgues, Tina was the first nurse to make a pot of coffee that wasn't liable to cause damage to visitors. He smiled agreeably once he had taken a sip and sat down in one of the two straight-back oak chairs in front of the coroner's cluttered desk, which was littered with various jars, many containing items best not asked about.

"I went to see Phil Pegler's widow," Sam said. "She wasn't surprised he was dead, but I did leave out most of the details. Amanda Pegler is a pretty lady who seems nice. It's a shame how things turned out for her. With her husband having been on state disability, at least she'll have enough insurance money to start over somewhere. She's determined to leave Silver City and I can't say that I blame her any, considering."

Whitlock snorted an agreement, keeping his attention glued to the novel he was reading.

"I haven't read Charles Dickens since Mrs. Bounds, my tenth-grade English teacher, forced me to," Sam said. "He wasn't as bad as I'd feared, but I can't recall being as engrossed in any of his stories as you appear to be."

Bryce Whitlock laid the book, pages splayed open, on his desk, put his feet to the floor and sat upright. "I take it you have never read *Bleak House*. You should, especially the part where the junk dealer, Mr. Krook, mysteriously bursts into flames, leaving behind only a pile of smoking ashes."

The sheriff's mouth dropped. "You're jerking my chain."

"Not at all. According to ole Charlie, spontaneous human combustion, as he terms it, is not that uncommon and has been recorded over centuries. I vaguely remember hearing about it during a lecture in medical school. It certainly merits more research. That could be what struck the Prophet."

Sam sipped his coffee. "This spontaneous human combustion thing, is it catching?"

The coroner gave a look of strained patience, like a grade-school teacher dealing with a particularly dense pupil. "It's quite rare, actually."

"You're sure?"

"Absolutely." Then Dr. Whitlock's eyebrows lowered and his features grew serious as he reached for a pack of Chesterfields, tapped out a cigarette and lit it. "Okay, tell me what happened."

"Take a gander at what's in that fire-extinguisher box." Sam nodded to the examination table. "The wildfire that was keeping the fire department busy today was apparently started by another case of this spontaneous human combustion. Freeman

Bates flagged me down on the road to show me what started the grassfire."

Dr. Whitlock stood, walked over and stared into the open fire-extinguisher box. After a moment he asked blandly, "Do you know who belonged to those feet?"

"No," Sinrod answered. "And as you can see there's nothing else to identify. It will likely take someone reporting a hunter missing. I did find a .410 Stevens shotgun just above where the fire started so I'd venture whoever the man was, he was out rabbit hunting when he caught on fire."

The coroner tapped ash from his cigarette. "I prescribe we retire to Archie's lounge for a few thinking drinks. This has been a long and odd day."

"Yeah," Sam agreed, grabbing up his hat. "That's without a doubt the best cure I've heard you come up with for quite a spell."

Chapter Eight

Archie's Tropicana Cocktail Lounge consisted of a large, one-story red-brick building that sat in the fork of the roads where highway 15 turned north to the near ghost town of Pinos Altos, seven miles distant.

One of Archie's attempts to emulate a tropical flavor consisted of a pair of palm trees planted on each side of the main entrance. The palms had frozen to death the first winter, only Archie kept insisting that they were simply "dormant" and would green up when the weather was agreeable. The fact that the trees had been "dormant" for six years caused the proprietor a lot of good-natured ribbing.

It was not the palm trees nor any other decor that caused Archie's to become the most popular tavern in Silver City for men to go and enjoy a relaxing drink. Archie Turnbull, a short, fat man with a permanent smile etched on his pock-marked face, prided himself in ferreting out and hiring the most attractive, alluring, tempting, and best of all, single cocktail waitresses in southern New Mexico. His biggest problem was keeping them from marrying one of the many lonely miners, who outnumbered women three to one in Grant County, then quitting their jobs.

Last year Dr. Bryce Whitlock had come perilously close to marrying one of the most dazzlingly beautiful women Archie had ever induced into coming to Silver City. Penelope Leathers was the girl's name and the enthralled coroner had fallen headlong for the luscious waitress. Whitlock had wasted scant time presenting Penelope with a two-carat diamond engagement ring which was enthusiastically accepted by the happy lady. Then the doctor's future bride asked to travel to Georgia and bring her aging and ill mother to New Mexico for their planned wedding. Dr. Whitlock had thought nothing of handing over money and happily given Penelope a thousand dollars cash to make the trip. He had not set eyes on her since.

A few days after Penelope's departure, Sam Sinrod had noticed the eye-catching engagement ring in the window of a notoriously crooked pawn shop where the seedy proprietor eventually disclosed the fact that Penelope Leathers had hocked it for fifty dollars. A small amount of detective work disclosed that the coroner's intended bride had a husband just released from prison in Colorado where he had finished serving three years for robbery.

Penelope Leathers had used Dr. Whitlock's "wedding" money to finance traveling to Colorado to meet her husband, Larry, and buy them a nice fast getaway car, a Ford V-8, just like John Dillinger had preferred. Sam never mentioned to his friend the fact that Penelope and Larry had robbed the Skyline Hotel before leaving Canon City, Colorado, where the prison was located. The duo had then left a crime trail across three states before finally being apprehended in Reno, Nevada. After robbing, of all things, an ice-delivery truck. Larry had not possessed enough good sense to buy gasoline and their Ford had coughed its last gasp only three blocks away, right in front of the police station.

It had taken the coroner several months before finally consenting to return to Archie's lounge. Only of late had the doctor begun to talk freely about the matter.

Sam Sinrod sat across from Bryce Whitlock in a shadowy back booth of Archie's where the table had been deeply carved with hundreds of names and initials from years of lovers pledging themselves to each other, however temporary the relationship.

Dr. Whitlock took a drink from a Carling Black Label beer. He rubbed the back of his hand across his mouth before setting the sweaty brown bottle on the table. "You know, Sam, I like this new waitress, Kathy. She really does seem nice."

Sam had furtively been studying the slender brunette while she made her rounds. Compared to Penelope Leathers' voluptuous form, this girl's bosom reminded him of two fried eggs tacked to a slab of wood. Kathy Webster did, however, have nice gams and a cute smile that was highlighted by a pair of sky-blue, Betty Boop–sized eyes. "Yeah, Archie gets only real pretty girls to work here."

"I can't help but wonder where Penelope is."

Sam knew with certainty where that scheming woman would be for the next ten to fifteen years, but his friend needed to recover from that sad episode. The less the subject of Penelope Leathers was visited, the better. "Dames are unpredictable as cats. Some are loyal while others will take food from you, then shred the hand that gave it to them. I wouldn't worry any on Penelope. I'm betting she's getting along right fine where she is."

Whitlock gave a slight sigh. "It *was* good of her to drop by your office to give back the ring and let you know that she was going to get back with her husband. I just wish she'd had the courage to tell me to my face. The money I can survive losing, but I honestly believed she loved me. The fact she was still married never came up."

Sam chewed on his lower lip. John Thayer at the pawn shop had been only too glad to hand over the ring and keep quiet about the matter once Sam had described the future he had in store if he didn't see things the way the sheriff wished. Besides, two hundred twenty dollars a month salary only stretched so far.

Sam thought for a moment and decided that wounds never healed if constantly picked at. "We have two dead people to explain away. I, for one, don't have a clue what to even write on the report, let alone tell that idiot editor at the newspaper. We never covered spontaneous human combustion when I went to sheriff school."

Dr. Whitlock gave a final glance to big-eyed Kathy then grabbed on to his bottle of beer with both hands. His voice was low when he said, "Barth suggested we attribute the deaths to an unknown but powerful fire-causing agent. I also think it would be wise to label both of the incidents as accidental. For the life of me, Sam, I can't fathom how they could possibly be homicides."

"Yep, I agree that it would be better to put these deaths down as unexplainable accidents. Hell, there's no way I could ever explain to anyone what happened even if these are actual cases of spontaneous human combustion."

Whitlock brought the beer to his mouth then hesitated. "Let's just hope no one else's goose gets cooked. That would be problems."

Sam Sinrod cocked his head in thought. "We can always run away from home and join the circus."

"I'll drink to that," Dr. Whitlock said before upending the bottle.

Chapter Nine

In the pressroom of the *Silver City Times,* senior editor Henry Miles Fossett sat in front of the massive Linotype machine that filled nearly an entire back wall of the brick building. He leaned back, flexed his long spindly fingers, cracked his bony knuckles and smiled evilly. This was the time of day he liked best of all, a time alone to tell the truth as seen through his eyes.

Grim midnight was two hours old. The only sound to be heard was the low keening wind that hooted and moaned through the eves like some tortured soul, eternally damned to the seventh circle of Dante's Hell. Shafts of yellow moonlight spearing through open windows undulated on the walls and floors with the passing of night clouds like fey spirits.

It was a time when ideas and words flowed free, a time when the truth could soar like an eagle unimpeded by narrow minds controlled by the forces of evil that were on a crusade to enslave and control the world.

Henry Fossett enjoyed telling how he had worked for many of the largest newspapers across the United States. And he had. At least for a week or two, until writing some *real* truth, not the watered-down version the Nazis wanted, then being fired for his efforts. That was their loss; he would build his message of truth from a smaller base, like the *Silver City Times* here in remote southwest New Mexico.

Henry Fossett was a man with a mission. The entire world was at war. The very survival of civilization was at stake. There were Nazis hiding in every city and town. Any gathering behind closed doors was a fertile breeding ground for sedition. It amazed him how precious few men of perception there were like him; men who could recognize traitors for what they were, before they struck.

Being perceptive was a cross Henry Fossett had to bear to save freedom. There was no doubt in his mind now, a Nazi plot was being hatched here in Silver City. Henry had paid a dollar to the lamebrain coroner's Mexican nurse for the privilege of viewing the ashes of another victim of Nazi atrocity. The price of vigilance meant paying people like the inherently stupid nurse and the dullard fire chief for information. Once the truth was known, thank God, those untrustworthy Mexicans would be sent home to stay. Freeman Bates, at least, wore a white skin. With proper indoctrination the New Order would find him useful.

And Henry Miles Fossett had learned at an early age the importance and methods of bringing people to the correct frame of mind. His bony back, shoulders and buttocks were a roadmap of long-healed scars that had been placed there by his own loving dad.

Henry had been slow to grasp the teachings of his Southern Baptist preacher father, Clell. But, as a good Christian, his father had thankfully not spared the rod and spoiled the child, as the Good Book admonished in plain, simple language. Henry Fossett owed the sanctity of his immortal soul to those painful lessons.

Not only had his father been a man of diligence when it came to saving souls from perdition, he was also a person of great foresight. Clell Fossett had attained the magnificent rank of Grand Wizard in the Tulsa, Oklahoma, chapter of the Ku Klux Klan.

The facts were plain to those willing to learn. There were

God's chosen people who wore a wrapping of pure white skin, akin to that of angels. Then there were niggers, Mexicans, chinks and Jews who, at best, were sluggish as cattle, soulless beings placed on God's earth by Satan to drain our resources and lay traps for the unwary.

Only Henry Fossett was no fool, not anymore. Yet, he reminded himself, Satan's temptations were subtle. He, like his sainted father, needed to show patience, for even Henry had once been caught up in the talons of the Devil's wiles. It had been another painful, though soul-saving lesson to be learned.

Henry had been in his second year of college. His family was *so* proud of him, the first of the Fossetts to garner an education past high school. All had been going well, his future assured, then the Devil had come to him in the seductive form of Lucinda Williams.

The girl had been given a shapely figure to turn men's heads. Lucinda's laugh was musical, her emerald eyes sparkled with promise. The way her firm young breasts filled out the charming summer dresses she wore was irresistible.

First she had tempted him into the abominable sin of dancing. Lucinda melded her body to his as they moved to the hypnotic beat of music. Music that had beats the same as those of a human heart, a trick of Satan's few knew. Then, as Henry's resistance against sin faded, he had allowed her to entice him into her bedroom.

The location of Lucinda's home should have been enough of a warning, but her assurances that her family was out of town for the weekend only added to the fire of lust in his loins, causing him to become weak in spirit.

In retrospect, the seductress's kinky, raven-black hair should have given warning, but Satan had hold of his heart and Henry Fossett, for the first and only time in his life, lay in bed with a harlot.

The next morning, after allowing himself to once again partake of forbidden fruit, he had noticed a picture of Lucinda's parents on a dresser as he made his way to the bathroom. *One of her parents was a Negro. She was a mulatto.*

Henry Fossett had rutted with a nigger. He had failed to resist temptation and sowed his precious Aryan seed inside of an animal. There was no worse sin a white man could have committed. He jumped into his clothes, yelled every epithet he knew at the startled girl who had seduced him and ran headlong back to his small room in the college dormitory.

After hours of praying and squeezing the Bible so hard blood trickled from his fingernails, Henry realized what he had to do. His pocketknife was a sharp Barlow. A few quick, determined slashes and the cause of his sinning was removed for all time.

The wonderful guiding voices that gave him direction had first begun when he was in the hospital recovering from blood loss. King David himself had come and ministered to him in a dream. The ancient biblical king and prophet of God had counseled him to tell people that he had been emasculated in an attack by three niggers. Not only did this spare Henry a stay in Vinita, where the Oklahoma state mental hospital was located, his furious father called a special meeting of the Klan. A few days later, a power pole became decorated with the dangling bodies of three Negroes. *A good start.*

Then, to help him on his mission to save the world from sin and corruption, Henry Fossett was blessed to have God send other voices to help guide and direct him.

Henry Fossett lit one of those slim, crooked cigars he enjoyed. They came from South Carolina, not some godless, heathen country like Cuba that was bent on destroying our way of life.

He hesitated to start typing. It had become painfully apparent to him that the truth, like some medicines, needed to be administered in small doses over a period of time.

Yet the cancer of Nazis and Fascists was spreading with terrible speed. The truth, Henry Fossett's truth, was sorely needed. The enemy had a new weapon that turned strong men into a heap of smoking ashes in mere seconds. He held no doubt this secret weapon was in the testing phase right here in the unlikely town of Silver City, New Mexico. Then he remembered the enemy was a cunning one, this was an *excellent* choice of place to carry out their nefarious schemes.

Only the Nazis had not counted on Henry Fossett. Not by a long shot. He took a puff on his cigar, grinned as the voice of Saint John whispered in his ear, and began to type.

Chapter Ten

A mile east of Archie's Tropicana Cocktail Lounge, in the Silver City fairgrounds, Doc Darby's traveling medicine show had drawn a sizeable crowd. On a brightly lit stage that folded out from the side of a shiny red Reo truck, a frail white-haired black man strummed a five-string banjo while Princess Nubia, a scantily clad "Indian" girl with long silky raven tresses, danced alluringly to enraptured men. To keep the kids entertained, Bubbles the clown juggled colorful balls.

Doc Darby kept smiling at the women, occasionally running a hand through his shoulder length silver hair. A man of experience, Doc knew which customers would likely part with a quarter to purchase a bottle of his patented, guaranteed, wrinkle-reducing, anti-aging Elixir of Life. He focused on the ladies because if he could convince them his potion reduced wrinkles, the men had no choice but to come up with money.

"Step forward, ladies," Darby said loudly with all the fever of a stump preacher out to save souls from Hell at any cost. "Observe the wonderful silky texture of Princess Nubia's skin. I know you believe this lady to be twenty, possibly twenty-five years old. My friends, I bring to you from the darkest jungles, at the headwaters of the mighty Amazon River, a miracle Methuselah would envy.

"At great peril to my life and limb I have brought back to civilization not only the formula for the Elixir of Life which I offer you here tonight, but proof of its worth in the form of a tribal chieftain's daughter. Yes, friends and neighbors, Princess Nubia here is lovely to behold, yet I tell you in all truth that when she was twenty years of age, Abraham Lincoln was still President of this great land!

"Yes, my friends, the lovely Princess Nubia is over one hundred years old. The Elixir of Life, which permeates and preserves not only the skin, but all internal organs as well, can and will reverse all matters of illness and aging, no matter how advanced or seemingly hopeless. And do I offer this miracle to you at five dollars a bottle, which is far less than it's worth? No, my wonderful friends in Silver City, I, from the goodness of my heart, offer to sell this boon of vibrant health to you for a mere quarter. Only twenty-five cents for a bottle will assure you ladies and gentlemen of long life and beauty. Five bottles can be purchased for only a dollar . . ."

Doc Darby hesitated in his spiel when the banjo player's music started going far out of tune. This was not too uncommon for old Parmenter Jones, who was becoming an increasing problem due to his tendency to get drunk before the shows were over. Darby made up his mind then and there to hire another banjo player as soon as possible.

Then a shrill scream ripped through the torrid night air. Doc Darby turned from the assembled crowd—something no successful showman ever did—to check out the source of the scream. It was Suzy Clay, or Princess Nubia as she was known to the public. Doc had been lucky enough to have had the dusky-skinned young Cherokee lady become enthralled with him over a year ago while he was performing a show in Oklahoma. Not only did Suzy's luscious form attract a large gathering of men, his offer to marry her at some future date kept him from having to pay her. Now for some odd reason, his main attraction had her hand pressed to her mouth and was staring wide-eyed at the white-haired banjo player who sat motionless on a stool in a far corner of the makeshift stage.

"Oh my God!" a voice from the audience cried out.

"Look at that!" another person yelled.

"The banjo player's on fire," a woman screamed. "He's burning up!"

Doc Darby forgot about selling his elixir and watched transfixed as Parmenter Jones' eyes were blown from their sockets by arrows of yellow flame. Smoke spewed from the old man's ears, nostrils and mouth.

Amid a swelling chorus of shrieks and cries, all present watched in horror as the banjo player's head seemed to melt into his thin torso, like hot wax from a candle. The flames grew in intensity, hissing like a provoked snake as internal organs and bone became incinerated. Within seconds, Parmenter Jones had turned into a pillar of bluish fire, sinking quickly downward through the wooden floor.

Doc Darby was the first to act. He grabbed fast onto Suzy Clay's arm as he simultaneously kicked Bubbles the clown from the stage to the ground.

"Run for your lives, folks," Darby yelled loudly. "There's a fifty-gallon gas tank under that man. It's going to blow sky-high any second!"

Darby, hauling the stunned Suzy Clay in tow, jumped from the stage. The duo had made around fifty feet or so when the medicine-show owner's predication was realized by a loud explosion that singed his long mane of silver hair as he shielded his lovely assistant from the effects of the fiery blast.

Chapter Eleven

"Now pard," Tasker Adams said cheerfully as they unloaded rolls of copper wire from the back of their Model A pickup to add to the burgeoning collection of various items they had "liberated" to sell. "A few more days like this one and we'll be set for winter."

"Winter can't come any too soon to suit me." Wesley Clinkenbeard wiped a bead of sweat from his forehead. "This is the hottest dad-burned summer I can ever remember suffering through." The old miner brightened. "But you are right about this being a good day. Dub hiring us to fix that hole in his floor was mighty good news, I'm here to tell you. Five bucks for a couple hours' work using materials we didn't have to pay for ain't bad at all."

Tasker grinned. "And it only got better when we saw that power company truck parked in front of Madame Millie's joint with no one around to watch over all of this valuable copper wire."

"I'm betting the fellow who was responsible for leaving that truck parked there wasn't inside to change a burned-out fuse."

"Nope," Tasker Adams affirmed. "And he's not going to own up to being anywhere near Millie's when he lost that wire off his truck either, that's a for sure."

Wesley eyed the ten cases of dynamite they had stacked up alongside that battered cylinder they had foolishly thought might be a meteor. "I'm telling you, pard, I'll be relieved as all get out to see all that old powder gone. Let's go out to the Santa Rita Mine soon and see if they'll buy it."

"There's a little zinc mine running near Fiero. I'd say we'd be better off going there. Those big companies tend to ask too many uncomfortable questions about where stuff comes from."

"Just so long as we get rid of it shortly—" His gaze focused on an odd-shaped dark spot on the floor. "Look at that, will you."

Tasker packed the last roll of wire inside the garage, carefully laid it against a case of dynamite then went to see what had taken his friend's attention.

"That wasn't there yesterday," Wesley said.

"It's only a pile of ash."

"Yeah, I know, but take a gander at its shape. The heap looks just like a big rat, tail and all."

"Now that you mention it, I reckon it does at that." Tasker shrugged. "So what?"

"I can't figure a rat-shaped pile of ashes appearing in our garage, that's what. With the Prophet burning up like he went and done, this sort of thing gives me the heebie-jeebies. I've never heard of either people or rats burning up without good reason."

"Wesley, my friend, I never figured on you to going screwball without working at it longer than you have." Tasker swiped his work boot and obliterated the ash pile. "Now it's all gone. Let's get the wood loaded up and dig out our carpenter tools. We've got a day of work facing us at Dub's bar, you know."

"Yeah, pard, I'm being plumb silly, I reckon. Not only do we get to spend the entire day in a bar, we're gonna be paid for it, to boot."

"There you go," Tasker said as they closed the garage door. "Things are coming our way, I can feel it in my bones."

A wan moon was hanging high in a gloomy midnight sky. Occasionally a gust of parching wind would shift the sheltering branches of the huge cottonwood trees that covered the cabin where Tasker Adams and Wesley Clinkenbeard slept, allowing a brief twinkling of stars to peek through the blackness.

The two old miners were lost in happy dreams, recalling younger days when the nights held promise and their lives stretched out before them like a long, long desert road. A time when their bodies were tough and the riches of King Midas lay just over the next mountain.

Inside of the adjoining garage, a huge brown Norway rat stood on its haunches and sniffed the air. The aroma was irresistible, yet unfamiliar. Using caution that had been bred into the species over millennia, the rat lowered itself to the floor, allowing its nose to guide it through the maze of strange objects that reeked of human scent, toward whatever was drawing it.

Suddenly the rat stopped dead still and bristled. Less than a foot away tiny flashes of light flickered and glowed against the dark like a gathering of diminutive lightning bugs. From a jagged crack in some type of long, round object, the rat's intended meal leaked slowly onto the wood floor.

The substance was one the sleek rodent had never encountered before, yet all of its senses told it to proceed. Food was available. A meal was something to never be passed up, no matter how unfamiliar or strange the nourishment might appear.

Slowly and carefully the rat approached the cylinder. It took a quick testing lap at the sparkling green substance. Scant seconds later the huge Norway rat was licking greedily away. The rodent's limited mind did register the fact that it was becoming quite hot in the stifling confines of the garage. But food was more important than comfort, and it continued to consume as much of the green substance as it could.

Chapter Twelve

Dr. Bryce Whitlock was summoning the courage to ask Kathy Webster, who by now had been transformed into the most gorgeous, charming, sweet and beautiful lady he had ever set eyes on, for a date when the wailing of multiple sirens on the highway in front of Archie's lounge seized his attention.

"There must have been a car wreck," Sam Sinrod said, looking bleary-eyed over a dozen empty brown beer bottles to a window that danced with flashing red and blue lights from passing emergency vehicles.

"I don't think so," Whitlock said, his brow creased with sudden concern. "The fire truck has a sound all its own. Those other sirens belong to the hospital ambulance and Burke Martin's cruiser, or I'll be surprised."

"If it is a car wreck, it must have been an awfully bad one."

Dr. Whitlock crushed out his cigarette and nodded in agreement. "Whatever's happened, they'll likely be needing the two of us."

"Indishpensable," Sam said with a slur. "It's times like these when I really wish we weren't such darn important people."

Whitlock blinked at lovely Kathy, who had appeared as if by magic.

"Dr. Whitlock," Kathy Webster said, her eyes were larger than the coroner remembered. "We just had an emergency phone call from the hospital. A medicine show caught fire and blew up at the fairgrounds. They said people were hurt and you may be needed." The waitress hesitated, then continued. "I must have misunderstood, but the nurse who called said a banjo player burnt up on stage and started the fire. That couldn't be right . . . could it?"

A suddenly sober Sheriff Sinrod looked up at the distraught cocktail waitress. His usual smile had been replaced with a frown of exasperation. "Do you know if there is a circus anywhere near here?"

"Not one that I've heard of," a thoroughly baffled Kathy Webster answered.

"I was afraid of that." Sam stood and hitched his gun belt. "Well, my good Dr. Watson, let's go catch some heat."

It was nearly four in the morning before the exhausted sheriff and coroner found time to sit at Dr. Whitlock's desk in the morgue and discuss the latest catastrophe without interference from others.

"This is why I keep my office in here," Whitlock said. "I tend to be left alone."

The sheriff glanced at an eyeball floating alongside a finger in a jar of formaldehyde on the coroner's desk and nodded in silent agreement. Dozens of other jars on shelves held the ingredients of nightmares. For good reason, everyone he knew avoided the morgue like the plague. There was a building pain in the top of his head. In all of Sam Sinrod's thirty years on this earth, he could not remember being as tired as he felt now. He wanted more than anything just to go to bed, pull the covers up around his neck and sleep for days.

"On the good side," Dr. Whitlock said cheerfully, "no one got worse than a singe when the truck's gas tank blew up. It would have been a lot worse if the medicine-show owner hadn't warned people to run."

Sam could not help but feel irritated at his friend's energy.

For some strange reason the doctor seemed immune to the effects of alcohol and lack of sleep. *Hell,* Sam thought, *the man perks up just before the sun rises. He's definitely not normal.*

"There wasn't even ashes we could identify left of the banjo player." The sheriff lit a cigar and thoughtfully blew a smoke ring to the ceiling. "Parmenter Jones was the dead man's name. Doc Darby said he didn't know of any relatives that need to be notified, but he'll check the car for any luggage he might have left in it, maybe find a letter or something."

"You mean *who* need to be notified."

Sam's head hurt worse when he nodded. Sometimes overeducated people could be a real pain, especially after a long trying day like this one had turned out to be. "Yeah, that's what I meant to say. It's been a rough day."

Dr. Whitlock tapped a Chesterfield from a pack. "Three cases of spontaneous human combustion in a period of twenty-four hours. That's most likely a record."

"*One* case is more of a record than we needed in Silver City, New Mexico."

"Yes, but the *why* is so intriguing. We both enjoy the novels of Sir Arthur Conan Doyle. I think Sherlock Holmes and Watson would be fascinated by this challenge."

And I think there were times Holmes seriously considered pummeling the crap out of Dr. Watson, Sam thought. "Henry Fossett is going to bandy this story to every newspaper across the country. I'll be under more pressure to solve these cases than anything I've encountered before. I might be a tad more optimistic after I get a few hours' sleep."

Dr. Whitlock glanced at the large oak Regulator clock ticking serenely on the wall over the stainless-steel autopsy table. "It is getting rather late. Why don't we catch some shut-eye and meet at Ellie's Diner for breakfast, say at seven. That way we can get an early start."

Sam Sinrod crushed out the fire from his cigar as he forced his legs to stand. "Yeah, why not? I'll be rested and fresh as a daisy by then, see you there."

The sheriff seriously wondered if it was worth the ten-minute drive to his house on Little Walnut Creek or whether to simply go to sleep in the front seat of the Ford Fordor. Then he noticed an unsavory burnt odor about his shirt and realized that a bath along with a shave and clean suit of clothes would be helpful to maintain his image as an elected public servant.

Sam stepped into the still torrid night. He relit his cigar, stared briefly at the glittering jeweled sky, then climbed into the cruiser, flicked on the lights and drove away into the darkness.

Chapter Thirteen

The red sky of morning was being pushed below the jagged eastern mountains by a blazing sun when Sheriff Sinrod pulled his cruiser to a stop in front of Ellie's Diner. Sam took out the gold Longines pocket watch he was inordinately proud of and smiled when he saw it was precisely seven a.m. Punctuality was a trait he prided himself on.

Two brief hours of sleep had worked wonders. The sheriff felt far more refreshed than he had expected. However, a particularly troubling and vivid dream of a long-forgotten incident when he was a boy of eight kept replaying in his mind like a stuck record.

Sam Sinrod had been born in Oklahoma and spent most of his young life in the town of Lone Wolf where his mother had worked as a school teacher to support the family while his father struggled in vain to hang on to a dry-land wheat farm during the terrible days of the Dust Bowl. This one particular evening he and some of his friends, including Timmie Martin, decided to build a fire to fry a big catfish they had caught from a small lake on the Martins' place.

It had been only a mudcat. Considering the red, murky water the fish had come out of, even at his young age Sam realized the catfish would taste like a mouthful of the countryside, yet he had voiced no opposition to the idea of cooking it.

The firewood they had gathered was damp from a rare afternoon thundershower and refused to burn. Boys being what they are, Timmie drained a gallon of gasoline from a tractor and doused some on a smouldering branch. The resulting unexpected explosion caused his startled friend to spill the rest of the gasoline down the front of his clothes, which instantly ignited.

Sam now clearly remembered a blazing Timmie Martin running wildly, beating futilely at the towering flames that engulfed him. Most of all he remembered the screams. Screams that human beings do not make . . . unless they are burning to death as Timmie Martin had done in Lone Wolf, Oklahoma, all those many years ago.

The sheriff shook his head, as if that could cast off an unwanted memory. He replaced his treasured watch into the front pocket of a freshly ironed and starched khaki shirt and walked inside Ellie's Diner to join Dr. Whitlock who was sitting alone sipping coffee at their usual table at a front window.

"Good morning, Sherlock," Whitlock said wearing a deadpan expression. "Have a cup of java and tell Dr. Watson what your plans are to keep the fine citizens and voters of Silver City safe and sound, at least until after the next election."

Sam scooted out a chair and frowned when he noticed it was the one with a wobbly leg that he disliked. He grabbed a sturdier chair from the next table, slid it over then sat down to join the doctor.

"First off, Watson, I have Doc Darby coming into my office to make a formal report on the medicine-show fire. District Attorney Norbert Pike will be there to make sure we at least get the paperwork filled out correctly. He's concerned about being reelected the same as we all are. We doubt the voters will simply stand still for us allowing people to catch on fire for no good reason like they've started doing. And for some reason we should have figured out by now."

The coroner smiled as Ellie Mason set a steamy cup of coffee in front of the sheriff, then coughed and pulled an order pad from her greasy apron.

"What'll you have, boys?" Ellie asked with a gravelly voice. The skinny restaurant owner chain-smoked Lucky Strikes in such disturbing numbers that it had caused even Dr. Whitlock, who dearly loved his Chesterfields, to advise her to cut back on smoking. It was to no avail. Ellie continued lighting one cigarette off the stub of another, consuming over four packs each day. With the price of cigarettes going to an unheard-of price of fifteen cents a pack, her habit had become an expensive one.

"Give me the fried ham steak, two eggs over easy, toast and hash-browns," Whitlock said.

Sam's nightmare was still all too vivid in his mind; he ordered a stack of pancakes smothered in chili. Once Ellie had hacked and coughed her way into the kitchen the sheriff said, "I wish she'd slow down on those cigarettes."

"Too much of anything isn't good for a person." Dr. Whitlock added a spoonful of sugar to his coffee, stirred it then poured some into the saucer to cool. "It was interesting to find that neither Phil Pegler nor the banjo player were smokers. We know for certain they both drank to some degree of excess, but they didn't carry matches or a lighter with them. That kills off a really good theory of how they could have caught fire."

"Come on, Doc, half of the people in Grant County pack around those things. A Zippo lighter doing its worst would only raise a good-sized blister. Nothing I know of would explain how anyone, smoker or not, could burn their way through the floor of a bar or the stage of a medicine show. Parmenter Jones just happened to be over the gas tank of the truck when he incinerated. We're just plenty lucky a lot of people didn't get bad hurt or killed when all of that gasoline exploded like it did."

"That's for sure," Dr. Whitlock slurped his coffee then set the saucer down, a quizzical expression on his face. "You still don't have any clue who belonged to those feet you found out at the brushfire?"

"No, but my guess is someone will be inquiring about a missing person sooner or later. The pair of boots and shotgun is all we have, to identify who it was. Let's hope that's enough."

"Perhaps when we find out who it was we can trace back their movements and actions. I'm hoping there will be some common thread of a connection to where they were, what they ate, and what they drank. Something, anything to give us a clue to why they caught on fire."

"I surely hope so." Sheriff Sinrod stirred two spoonfuls of cream into his coffee. "Did Charles Dickens say anything in that book of his as to why the junk dealer, Krook, got burned up by spontaneous human combustion?"

Dr. Whitlock chuckled. "Dickens was a fiction writer, so I wouldn't give much credence to anything he said, but he simply wrote around the event as if people burning up were common as catching a cold." He refilled the saucer. "I'll pore over some medical books and then I'll give the state medical examiner in Santa Fe a call. I'll see what Dr. Rogers thinks we could do to at least appear to be making an investigation. There's going to be a lot of questions asked of us, and they're going to hit really soon."

Sam Sinrod turned to stare at the window where piercing shafts of sunlight signaled another hot dry day was in the offing. "I wish this drought would end."

"We all do. With a world war on and everything being rationed, even food, folks need to raise as big of a victory garden as they can. That's hard to do without water. The forest north of here is a tinderbox. Fish in the Gila River are growing legs so they can walk to a stream that still has water in it."

Ellie Mason came coughing and hacking her way from the kitchen carrying their breakfasts, a cigarette dangling from one side of her mouth.

Dr. Whitlock dove into his food with obvious relish. Sam found the repulsive odor of fried meat had upset his appetite and only picked listlessly at his huge stack of piping hot sourdough pancakes that were buried under a mound of red-hot chili.

Chapter Fourteen

A chubby man wearing a smudged and tattered clown costume, puffing furiously on the stub of a cigar, was sitting on a bench outside of the sheriff's office when Sam Sinrod arrived.

"I'm Bubbles," the man in the clown suit said, unasked. "All my clothes got burnt up when the medicine-show truck exploded last night. I got the only car so I had to drive Doc Darby and Suzy over here." The man rubbed his stubble-bearded cherubic face. "I sure hope Doc has enough money stuck back so that I can buy some other clothes to wear. Folks look at me funny when I run around dressed like this."

"Yeah," Sheriff Sinrod agreed and nodded as he stepped through the door to his office. "I suppose they do."

Norbert Pike sat tall at one end of Sam's desk, holding a note pad and tablet in his lap. At seven feet two inches, he had no choice but to sit tall. The district attorney of Grant County for nearly thirty years, Norbert's favorite saying was that in his domain, "No one is above the law."

"Good morning Sam," the district attorney said, motioning with a head wag to a thin older man who held the hand of a raven-haired young lady who sat by his side. "This is Doc Darby, the medicine-show owner and"—he consulted his notes—"Princess Nubia, also known as Suzy Clay. They were already here when I showed up nearly an hour ago."

The thin man stood to shake the sheriff's hand. Curled patches in his silver mane showed his hair had obviously been fairly well singed in last night's fire. "My name is Preston Darby, but most folks call me Doc. I own . . . well, I used to own the traveling medicine show that burnt up." Darby sighed. "Suzy and I lived in the truck. So did Parmenter Jones and Bubbles. Everything we had was lost in the fire."

Sam Sinrod forced his eyes from Suzy Clay's enticing figure that was still wrapped in a very skimpy halter top and daringly short leather skirt. He took a deep breath to regain his focus. "I'm sorry for your loss, but under the, ah . . . strange circumstances surrounding the death of Parmenter Jones, you must understand our need to investigate this matter thoroughly."

"I certainly do, Sheriff," Darby said as Sam Sinrod walked around the district attorney and took the chair behind his desk. "I've been doing medicine shows all of my life . . . my father had one. Believe me, I've never even *heard* of anything happening like what caused poor Parmenter to catch on fire like he did last night."

Norbert Pike said, "This Elixir of Life you sell, what's in it?"

Doc Darby shrugged. "I sell, or rather sold, entertainment. The Elixir of Life is no secret. Mainly it's the cheapest Mexican Mescal I can find, along with enough tobacco juice and turpentine to make it look, smell and taste bad. People don't believe any medicine works unless it tastes awful to drink."

Sheriff Sinrod found his gaze drifting to Suzy Clay. "I understand that the banjo player was known as a heavy drinker. Did Mr. Jones ever drink any of this elixir?"

"No sir, he never got *that* desperate," Doc Darby said firmly. "Parmenter Jones had been known to strain wood alcohol through a loaf of bread and drink it when he got really hard up, but he helped me buy the ingredients, mix and bottle my elixir so he knew everything that went in it. The man was a drunk, not an idiot."

"Choking down a spoonful or two is about as much as anyone

can manage, no matter how desperate they are," Suzy Clay added.

Sam Sinrod leaned back in his oak swivel chair and laced his fingers behind his head. "Mr. Darby, I suppose you are aware that aside from Parmenter Jones, we've had two other people burn up from what the coroner is calling, at least until we get a better handle on the problem, 'spontaneous human combustion.' There may be something in common those three came in contact with. We only want to eliminate the elixir you are selling as the cause of death."

"You know," Suzy volunteered, "poor Parmenter burned up just like that man did in *Bleak House*. That was a case of spontaneous human combustion."

"Yes, I remember reading that book, it was a novel by Charles Dickens," Norbert Pike said in agreement. "The fellow who burnt up, his name was Krook."

"The junk dealer," Doc Darby added with a nod. "A pile of ashes were all they found left of him."

Sam Sinrod began studying his appointment calendar. It appeared more and more that he was the only person in New Mexico who hadn't made a career out of reading Charles Dickens.

He took a moment to think about the situation before speaking. There did not seem to be any possible way Phil Pegler could have had contact with the medicine show. The Prophet lived in a cave and only came into town to drink beer and eat at Dub's Place. Doc Darby had been in Silver City only one day and the entire troop had come in from Arizona. The showman had lost everything in the fire. Darby seemed truthful and honestly bewildered as everyone else over what had happened. Sam could see no reason to continue this interrogation. "The clown outside mentioned he hoped there was money for him to buy some new clothes."

Darby's face twisted in anguish. "I owe Bubbles twelve dollars and I wish to heaven I had it to pay him. Every dollar of the show money, all nine hundred bucks of it, was kept in a strong wood box I built into the floor of the truck. You know, I suppose I should've made it out of steel, like a small metal safe. But I reckon it's a bit late to think about that now."

The sheriff thought for a moment before pulling a pen from his shirt pocket and scribbling a note. Then he reached across the desk and handed it to Doc Darby. "Show this to Father Mondragon over at Saint Mary's Church. It's just a couple of blocks north of here. The priest is an understanding man and he helps out a lot of people who are down on their luck. Father Mondragon will give you folks clothes, meals, and a place to stay for a while. I'd also appreciate it if you folks would stick around town for another day or so, perhaps by then we can have a handle on why those fellows caught fire."

Doc Darby and Suzy Clay stood, said thanks and their goodbyes. All Sam Sinrod could do was nod. The closeness of the scantily clad Indian girl had effectively silenced the sheriff.

"I've been prosecuting criminals for thirty years," Norbert Pike said after the medicine-show owner and his girlfriend had gone. "Preston Darby's no more of a doctor than I am, but I don't believe he's a bad person. I'd stake my reputation that he's just as puzzled by all this as we are."

"Those are my feelings, too, Norbert, but I need some answers—"

A dark shadow washed across the sheriff's desk. Sam's wide eyes looked to the now-somber open doorway.

"Oh shit," he gasped.

Chapter Fifteen

Henry Miles Fossett leaned forward in his chair and pored over a proof copy of the *Silver City Times* with the practiced eye of an editor. The paper would not be delivered to the public until late this afternoon, he still had time to make this a special edition and change copy. This is what he sincerely wanted to do. In the past however, he had occasionally printed too much truth at one time and caused himself problems. The masses had to be educated slowly, much to his displeasure.

The blatant Nazi attack of last evening on an innocent icon of American culture, the traveling medicine show, was a difficult story not to blast across headlines. But Henry Fossett knew he lacked any concrete evidence to connect those Godless bloodthirsty Germans with the incident, yet in his heart he knew them to be guilty without doubt.

The good, decent and hardworking citizens of a God-fearing country like the United States of America did not go and burst into flames unless they were victims of some nefarious plot. And it was well-known fact that the Nazis were fervently working on secret weapons. There were also plenty of heathen Hitlerites right here in Silver City who were undoubtedly the cause of these terrible deeds.

Otto Ludwig, the owner of the local slaughterhouse, had difficulty even speaking the language of the country that now nurtured him and his family. Anton Drehr, a hulking Prussian with a low brow, a definite indication of Simian origin, ran the local hardware store only a mere block from where he sat. Ed Von Gendren was entrusted with delivering milk and cheese to be consumed by trusting women and children. *Unbelievable stupidity.*

The list of the untrustworthy went on and on. Even the sheriff was most likely a Nazi. Henry Fossett had studied on this but he was not certain what nationality the surname Sinrod signified. It did not, however, appear to represent any decent, God-fearing country he was aware of. The coroner used the honest person's name of Whitlock, but Fossett held his doubts. The man's eyes were set closer together than they were on a true Aryan. Perhaps his bloodline had become tainted by interbreeding with an inferior race. Yes, this had to be the case. Without question the doctor was a beer-drinking idiot.

Three Dead in Separate Fires of Suspicious Origin, the headlines read. Henry felt good about the photographs, especially the eye-catching one of the pair of boots that still held charred feet. The caption read in thirty-point type: *County Sheriff Sinrod unable to explain how incinerated men left few remains.* The way the blackened stubs of bone stuck out was downright wonderful. He imagined the stupid coroner would be visiting soon to ask him how he obtained access to the morgue. The truth would likely cause a certain Mexican nurse to be out of a job.

Henry Fossett grinned thinly at the prospect. The truth was his stock in trade and he would tell the truth to the coroner about paying money to be shown the garish remains. There were far too many Mexicans in New Mexico anyway. Perhaps soon they all would be sent packing back to their homeland. The stupid nurse would simply be a good start.

He sighed and grabbed up a copy with bony fingers and folded it to fit in a large envelope already addressed to the *Santa Fe Journal.* He simply had to postpone sending out more truth in this issue, no matter how distressful it was to tarry in his task. There were dozens of other envelopes destined for all of the major newspapers from the *New York Times* to the *Denver Post* and *San Francisco Chronicle.*

Perhaps, Henry fervently hoped, some other editors might be as astute as he and join in printing the wake-up call that sedition was afoot. Time was of the essence. Truth and the white Anglo-American way of life were at stake. And the forces of evil never slept.

Henry Fossett glanced up at the clock. He hurriedly folded the rest of the newspapers into envelopes. He had less than twenty minutes to get his messages in today's mail. A man out to save his country could ill afford to be tardy.

Chapter Sixteen

The dark shadow filling Sam Sinrod's office doorway hardened into the scowling hulk of Hester Guttman. Norbert Pike tried unsuccessfully to scrunch himself into invisibility as the matron strode to the sheriff's desk, her black cape fluttering like a wounded bat.

Long a legend in Grant County, Hester Guttman claimed to be a descendent of the famous saloon-busting prohibitionist, Carry Nation. She was constantly rallying to close all of the bars and to ban dancing, even at the high-school prom. Every election there were numerous amendments on the ballot—fostered by her to curtail sin—that were always soundly defeated. At last count, nine Southern Baptist preachers had resigned from the church she attended and left Silver City simply to get away from her. Drinking men claimed you could tell when Hester was about by listening for dogs howling.

"Sheriff, Mr. Pike," Hester Guttman said meekly, surprising both men. Normally her voice was as menacing as a growl from the somber maw of a cave. "I need your help."

"What can we do for you, ma'am?" Sam asked after taking a moment to study on his reply and compose himself.

"It's about my poor husband, Percy, Sheriff. He did not come home last night and I'm beside myself with worry. Percy has never done anything like this before."

Sam Sinrod swallowed hard to keep from saying anything he would regret later, like the first thing that came to mind. Good sense would be all of the incentive most men would need to start running away from that woman and not slow down for three states.

Percy Guttman was a retired pharmacist and well respected in the community. The fact that such an educated, sweet-natured little man went and made such a monumental mistake as marrying Hester, gave a lot citizens incentive not to take a chance on being a teetotaler like Percy. It was obvious to any thinking person that too much sobriety could definitely warp a man's judgment.

"Ma'am, uh, Mrs. Guttman," Sam finally managed to say. "Are you wanting to file a missing person's report."

"I didn't expect you to be such an idiot, Sheriff Sinrod. I would not be here if I did not want to file a report. I expect you to do your job or I shall form a recall election, sir!"

Sam nodded and began fishing through his desk for the appropriate form. He felt better now that Hester's demeanor had returned to normal. Also he knew that any petition started by her would only garner him more votes.

"When was the last time you saw your husband?" Norbert asked with concern.

"Yesterday morning," Hester said. "We ate breakfast together. I made him a nice stack of pancakes with maple syrup . . . Percy simply loves real Vermont maple syrup . . . then he went to the closet, took out his gun and said he was going rabbit hunting. I surely hope he has not suffered from an accident such as a broken leg and laid out in that terrible desert overnight."

The district attorney and sheriff exchanged knowing glances. "Mrs. Guttman," Sam Sinrod's words were measured, cautious. "Did you husband take along a shotgun?"

"Of course he did. Percy simply loves rabbit stew the way I fix it for him with lots of turnips, celery and wild sage. I bought him a Stevens .410-gauge double-barreled shotgun for Christmas the first year of our marriage. Rabbits are decidedly difficult to hit with a rifle for a man with poor eyesight like my Percy suffers from. He is badly nearsighted."

Sam thought the inside of his lip was likely bleeding from where he had been biting it. "Mrs. Guttman, would you recognize the boots he wore when he left that morning?"

"Of course I would. I bought them for him. I have to buy all of Percy's clothes. That man simply has no taste at all when it comes to his attire. He would embarrass me to no end if I did not see to the appropriateness of his apparel. But to answer your ridiculous question, certainly I would recognize Percy's boots—" A pall washed across Hester Guttman's face. "Oh my dear God, something terrible has happened to him."

Norbert Pike stood and placed a comforting hand on Hester's shoulder. "If you would be so kind as to please accompany us to the morgue, we'll know if the worst has happened."

Hester Guttman daubed a white silk handkerchief to teary eyes as she kept her gaze on the pair of boots setting in a box of gray ashes. "My poor Percy being completely burned up in a brushfire. I simply cannot understand how such a horrible thing such as that could have happened. But the Stevens shotgun you showed me is his and there is no doubt whatsoever those are my husband's boots."

Dr. Whitlock stepped to the examination table and draped a towel over the box. He felt the burnt stubs of bones protruding from the boots might be a distraction to the newly widowed Hester and he desperately wanted some questions answered. "I hate to ask at a time like this, but Mrs. Guttman did your husband smoke?"

"Of course he did not," Hester spat. "My Percy was a true gentleman and I saw to it that he stayed one. Only crude people indulge in such a filthy habit as filling a room with smoke."

The coroner crushed out a stub of cigarette. "Mrs. Guttman, ma'am, I don't know how to bring this up delicately, so I apologize in advance if this offends you. It appears, however, that your husband's burning up is what started the brushfire. Before you answer me, you should be aware there are two other cases where dozens of witnesses saw the people catch fire right in front of them."

Hester slumped slightly and gave a sigh. "Yes of course, I have heard about this. At the last meeting of my garden club we talked about nothing else. That degenerate man in the bar who caught on fire had obviously saturated his body with alcohol like that awful Krook fellow did in *Bleak House,* which adequately explains his being immolated by God's cleansing fire. I do not know anything about the banjo player, but I know something about musicians. If he was a drinking man he only got his just comeuppance. I assure you Dr. Whitlock, that never a single drop of liquor passed my Percy's lips. You must look to other causes, my good man."

Sam Sinrod spoke up, "To be honest, Mrs. Guttman, we don't have a clue as to why *any* of those people caught fire. We were hoping you might be able to help us."

"Explaining my husband's death is *your* job, Sheriff," Hester growled. She turned to leave then hesitated. "The governor of this great state, Herschell Castle, is my personal friend and a fellow Christian. I shall phone him immediately and have him send some *competent* investigators to Silver City. I also expect my poor Percy's remains to be delivered to Thorton's Funeral Home without delay. Years ago I bought and paid for a fine expensive mahogany coffin with solid brass handles and a lining of pure blue silk. His remains *will* be buried in it."

The sheriff started to say something but Hester's slamming the door as she left froze the words on his lips.

Dr. Whitlock lit another cigarette. "Well, I can't say *that* was a lot of help."

The district attorney shrugged. "In my opinion we ought to go check out what Ellie's got for today's lunch special. With all of the good government help we'll have coming our way, I can't figure out why we need to worry ourselves over the matter. We can start blaming the folks in Santa Fe for not knowing how to stop what's going on."

"You fellows go ahead," Sam said. His appetite had yet to return and he did not want to endure the smell of frying meat. "I need to get back to the office to start putting all of my paperwork in order. Company's coming y'know."

The corner glanced over his shoulder at the towel-covered box. "I hope whoever comes from Santa Fe don't think they're hot stuff. We've had more than enough of those to go around."

When Sam pulled his cruiser into the parking lot beside the station house he noticed Payatt Hae was across the street filling a metal water tank in the back of his battered old pickup with a well-patched garden hose. The city outlets were there for people who were out of water and had paid a dollar to the town to purchase a thousand gallons. There were no meters or anyone around to check who came in or out or how often they came; the entire affair was run on trust.

A drought hard enough to dry up old Payatt's spring would set a record for Grant County, if that were the case. There was always the possibility the venerable Apache could be hauling water for a friend. Anyway, it had been a long while since Sam had visited with him. Frank Hae, Payatt's grandson, had been a good deputy. It had been a loss to the department when he left to join the Army. The sheriff pulled his hat down firm to keep a hot gust of wind from propelling it to Texas and crossed the dusty street.

"I hope your spring hasn't petered out," Sam said. He had learned early on that Indians measured time by a different clock than anyone else. Waiting for them to initiate a conversation could require a calendar.

"It is dry."

Sam Sinrod shook his head sadly. "Sorry to hear that, but a lot of folks' wells are going dry from this drought. Maybe we'll get some rain soon."

"The spring is not the problem. The white-eyes who built that windmill are taking all of my water." Payatt leaned on the cool tank to eye the sheriff. "The water is mine. Will you put the ones who stole my water in jail?"

"Now Mr. Hae, we've talked about this before. That windmill is on government land and the company that leases the property pays them for the right to use it. They have got a legal license to pump that water for their livestock."

"It does not matter. The Great God, *Usen,* is throwing fireballs at that windmill from Heaven. I will dance a *Gahe* to help his aim. Once he hits it, no problem."

Sam cocked his head. "Are you saying something like a meteor struck near the mill?"

"It was a fireball from Heaven, as I have said." The old Indian tapped on the tank with his fist to determine the water level. "The Great God only missed it by a few feet, which was a shame. If the god's aim had been better, I would not be having to haul this water."

"I'm surprised a fireball didn't catch the countryside on fire, dry as it is."

"*Usen* would not allow such a thing. He only wished to smash that windmill."

Sam thought on the matter. If Payatt Hae said he saw something flaming fall from the sky, there was no questioning the occurrence. And there *had* been unusually high numbers of aircraft flying about lately. The new White Sands Military Base was not a far distance to the east. Whatever had struck near the windmill could have been a small aircraft or possibly something that had broken loose from one and crashed to earth. He should at least go examine the area for wreckage.

"I'd better go check that area out. There might have been something fall out there that needs to be reported to the Army."

Payatt Hae's expression remained chiseled of stone. "The fire was from *Usen*'s hand. Go and look, but do not go at night. I would not like for you to be at that windmill when the Great God finally hits it."

"You take care," Sam said, then remembered to ask. "How's Frank?"

"He is in South Pacific. We had a letter from him last week. Do you know it never snows in that strange land. I do not think a place where it never snows would be worth much. Perhaps the Japanese should be allowed to keep it."

"I'm glad Frank is well. Next time you write, be sure to tell him he still has his job as a deputy once this war is over."

"I will." Payatt thumped the tank again. "It is full." He shut off the valve, coiled the hose neatly, hopped in his old truck and drove off without uttering another word.

Chapter Seventeen

Dr. Bryce Whitlock and Sam Sinrod trudged side by side up the powder-dry grade to the windmill beneath a cloudless, merciless afternoon sun. The road they walked up was steep and littered with sharp rocks, a sure invitation to a blowout, which was why they had left the car parked on the main road. The tires on Sam's Ford cruiser had been patched so many times that Vern Jensen at the garage complained that he was running out of places to put air. With rubber being rationed for the war effort, a new set of tires was a dreamed-of luxury, even for a county sheriff's cruiser.

A stinging lizard, so named because when the harmless little creatures ran they carried their tails high, like a scorpion, scampered across the road in front of them kicking up tiny clouds of dust with its spindly feet.

The coroner stopped to catch his breath. One of the irritating effects of living with diabetes was occasional fatigue. "Did you know that down in Lordsburg it's so dry that the lizards have started packing canteens."

"If I lived in Lordsburg, I would just as soon croak. That country down there tends to make Hell look like the Promised Land." Sam Sinrod hesitated a moment to swat a green fly out of his ear. "The only thing good I can say about the place is, it's in another county."

Whitlock gave an evil grin. "Did 'ems eat at the Plaza again?"

Sam sighed. "Last week I had to go down and testify on a

goat-rustling case. The guy went and pleaded guilty while I was driving down there so I decided to have breakfast before heading back. I never knew germs could infest fried eggs and sausage, but those Lordsburg germs are tougher than most. Before I hit the county line, my stomach started rumbling. I had the runs for two days."

"That'll teach you to tempt fate. Even starving, stray dogs that want to see another sunrise give that place a wide berth. Big Sally Mounds waiting tables is the only reason any man goes there."

"She surely does have a big set of jugs all right, but some shows don't come close to being worth the ticket price." Sam squinted in the bright sun as he looked toward the distant windmill. "Old Payatt Hae was sure right about something burning up there. I can see the charred area from here."

"Well, let's get to hoofing and see the reason we came out here on such a pleasant afternoon as this. It can't be over a hundred degrees in the shade, if there was any shade."

"Yep." Sam kicked a rock with the toe of his boot and started for the clanking windmill. "The climate here's a sight better than Lordsburg, that's for sure."

The coroner took a blackened piece of metal from a kitchen sieve he had brought along in a valise containing items he thought useful to forensic field work. He studied it carefully using a hand magnifying glass. "You said the old Apache claims one of his gods threw a fireball at that windmill?"

"It was the Earth God, *Usen.* Payatt also says he plans to keep beseeching *Usen* to keep at it until the windmill is flattened. He believes the mill sucking water out of the ground dried up his spring." Sam walked over and looked once again into the insect-infested, nearly dry rock tank. He sighed and shook his head sadly. "But the fact of the matter is, this well's barely pumping enough water to keep from wearing out the leathers, let alone support any livestock. I'd venture the company has already moved their cattle, which explains why we haven't seen any, but they should shut the windmill off."

"This *Usen* chap," Whitlock said, keeping his attention focused on the jagged piece of metal he had found, "his initials wouldn't be U.S.A. by chance?"

"Huh?" Sam snorted.

"Whatever made this crater came stamped 'USA' so I would look to the government rather than Heaven or the Apache for its source."

The sheriff cocked his hat to keep the sun out of his eyes as he looked over the shallow hole that had been blasted into the hillside. "Whatever it was sure wasn't very big or it got destroyed when it smashed in. My guess is something possibly might have fallen off of an airplane and crashed here. The Army's doing a lot of testing these days, they may not realize they even lost whatever it was. I doubt a little incident like this would warrant them even bothering to tell us about it."

"We should be thankful it wasn't a bomb or anything that might have caught the countryside on fire. The whole damn county is nothing but a tinderbox. I say we head back to town, take care of what we have to then go meet up at Archie's lounge. That excelsior air cooler he put in makes it a mighty pleasant place to drink a beer."

"There's nothing I can see to keep us here." Sam glanced up one last time at the clanking windmill. "You know it's too bad it actually wasn't an errant bomb. That would have put a smile on old Payatt Hae's face." He cocked his head in thought for a moment. "Well, it would have made him happy anyway. Let's get going, the weather's not getting any cooler and if I remember correctly, it's your turn to buy the first beer."

★ ★ ★ ★ ★

When the coroner returned to his office in the morgue, he found his secretary, Tina, holding a copy of the *Silver City Times.* For some reason she seemed to be fighting back tears.

"I agree that new editor leaves a lot to be desired," Whitlock said cheerfully, hoping to lighten whatever the situation was. "Henry Fossett's writing has brought tears to my eyes on several occasions, too."

"I am so very sorry, Dr. Whitlock," Tina said, her voice choked with imprisoned sobs. "Mr. Fossett came over and asked to see the remains of those people who burned up all by themselves. Mister Fossett was so grateful when I agreed to let him inside that he gave us a dollar, which I put in the coffee kitty." She laid out the newspaper to face the doctor. "This article is awful. If I had known that man would write something like this, I would never have let him in. Now I will lose my job."

Whitlock grabbed up the paper, frowned at the grisly photograph on the cover and scanned the story before tossing the paper back on the desk. "The sheriff and I will go and have ourselves a little chat with Mr. Fossett. You did nothing wrong, Tina, and your job's safe. I told you to be open with the press when you came to work here. But when it comes to Henry Fossett, I think we'd best give him the bum's rush next time he shows his face here."

"Señor," Tina Ortega's voice turned fiery enough to melt lead. "If that *cabrón* comes here again, I will rip out his *huevos* with my bare hands and cram them down his throat. And then I will become nasty."

The coroner grinned in spite of the fact that the editor had surely sent copies of the newspaper all over the state and who knew where else, likely causing more publicity and trouble than even Hester Guttman was planning.

"That sounds good to me," Dr. Whitlock said on his way into

the morgue where it was agreeably cool to smoke a cigarette while trying to decide how to handle the storm that was certainly heading their way.

When Sam Sinrod returned to his red-brick office adjacent to the courthouse, he found in the waiting room a short, fat man who wore his brown hair slicked to his head with copious amounts of what smelled like Wildroot hair oil. The sheriff knew without asking where the man was from. In spite of the fact that the state capital of Santa Fe was three hundred miles distant, officials coming to cause him problems seemed to make the trek faster than anyone would expect. This fellow, however, had set a new record.

"You must be Sheriff Sinrod?" the man asked, standing and extending his hand. "I have been waiting for nearly a half hour for you to return."

"Yes sir, I do get busy on occasion. How may I help you?" Sam fought an urge to wipe his hand.

"My name is Roan Walker. I'm an officer assigned to the State Police headquarters in Santa Fe. I'm the chief arson investigator. Governor Castle personally called and asked me to come to Silver City and aid in your investigation of some rather strange cases of people going up in flames. I understand you have had three instances of that happening, hereabouts."

"I'll be happy to share with you the files and any information our office has obtained. We are all hoping you can explain what causes cases of spontaneous human combustion. These people burned up just like the junk dealer, Krook, did in Charles Dickens' *Bleak House.*"

Roan Walker blinked. "I wasn't aware Dickens had ever written about something like that."

Sinrod gave a sly grin. "There's a lot of knowledge to be gained from reading great literature, Officer Walker. I'll have a copy of our files sent to your room. I must say you made the trip here so fast you must have flown."

"Actually, Sheriff, I did. The state has a Ford Tri-Motor airplane available for use in special cases. This is certainly one of them."

Thank you, Hester Guttman, Sam thought. "I shall be glad to drive you over to the Copper Mountain Hotel and see you settled in. I'm sure you are tired from the trip."

"That would be good of you. I do wish to take the files with me so I can study them tonight. I have a couple of ah . . . associates driving down, so the use of a car will not be necessary."

The thought of two more state policemen coming to meddle in his affairs washed the smile from Sam's face. He did not even have a car available for Roan Walker's use, but decided telling him this might cause a tatter in their budding relationship. "I'll send a deputy by later with the files. It will take me a bit of time to make certain they're complete. Why don't you let me help with your luggage. The Copper Mountain has installed some of those evaporation coolers and it's a sight more pleasant there."

Roan Walker nodded. "I must say, Sheriff, that I am impressed by your helpful attitude. Generally, small-town lawmen do not appreciate having *professionals* assist them with an investigation."

Sam thought the inside of his lip was bleeding again from his biting on it. "Oh, on the contrary. We are all *so* glad you're here. There's more than enough heat on this case to share." He held up a copy of the *Silver City Times* that he had picked up at the drugstore when he had stopped to enjoy a frosty cool phosphate.

The sheriff rolled up the newspaper and tucked it under the officer's arm. "I'll be pleased as punch to tell any and all reporters who ask that Roan Walker, chief arson investigator of the New Mexico State Police is in charge of the investigation, not me. Now, how about letting me drive you and all of that heavy luggage of yours over to the hotel."

Chapter Eighteen

Bryce Whitlock tapped a fresh Chesterfield from a pack, lit a cigarette with his Zippo, clicked the top closed and leaned back in the cool wood booth of Archie's Tropicana Cocktail Lounge. He blew a smoke ring as he eyed Kathy Webster's shapely derriere wiggle down the aisle.

"You really should just go ahead and get it out of your system, Doc." Sam Sinrod was slowly spinning a sweaty bottle of Carling Black Label beer as he spoke. "Just keep in mind that you're under no obligation to marry a girl simply because you ask her out on a date. The whole idea is to see how well you get along together."

"The good sheriff attempts to see beyond the pale."

Sam moaned. "Spouting philosophy in a workingman's bar when there's a pretty lady about. Now that just beats all. I'm glad I didn't go and wreck my common sense by lollygagging around some college for years. No sir, I took an honest job right out of high school."

The coroner's expression turned thoughtful. "I wasn't aware that driving a beer truck during prohibition was exactly honest work. But I suppose it did serve to nurture the morals necessary to becoming a lawman."

"You can't round them up if you don't know how they think."

"I'll drink to that," Whitlock said grabbing up his beer. "Hell, considering the way things have been going lately, I'd drink to darn near anything."

Sam Sinrod and the coroner sat in heavy silence for several long moments. Both of them knew it was time to move on to serious matters. The uproar over three unexplained cases of spontaneous human combustion was building like an approaching thunderstorm. Henry Fossett's muckraking newspaper writing, coupled with Hester Guttman's political connections had colluded to focus a spotlight of publicity on them that would not go away anytime soon.

"This country needs a rainstorm," Sam said somewhat contritely. "What we're getting is a shitstorm."

"I don't know why these people couldn't have had the decency to make an ash out of themselves some place other than here in Grant County." Dr. Whitlock finished his beer and held the empty bottle up to catch Kathy's attention. "My friend, Dr. Rogers in Santa Fe, called to tell me the attorney general is threatening to send him down here if I don't come up with some answers that will close these cases, especially Percy Guttman's, real soon."

"Lordsburg would've been a much better place for an outbreak of spontaneous human combustion," Sam said. "They could've swept all of the evidence under a rug down there and no one would ever notice." His expression turned grim. "An officer by the name of Roan Walker is here from the State Police. He told me a couple of other state boys are driving down. Walker is the chief arson investigator, they flew him here in an airplane."

"In all honesty, Sam, I'm hoping someone from the capital *can* show up and explain what happened. I'm stumped and the medical books don't even try to explain people burning up by themselves. Dr. Rogers thought it might relate to a buildup of alcohol in the system. But we all know Percy Guttman didn't drink, which shoots down that theory."

The sheriff blinked. "I wonder if Percy could have been one of those closet drinkers. Considering who he was married to, it would seem to be a real possibility."

"No one could blame him, that's a for sure, but how can we ever prove it? Hester wouldn't believe us even if we found his stash with his name written on the bottles. No, Sam, whatever the cause, we'll need more than a theory—"

Kathy Webster stopped the conversation when she glided up and batted her saucer-sized eyes at Dr. Whitlock. "My, but you boys are thirsty this evening. I read that newspaper story about how those awful Nazis are behind those poor people burning up like they did. I hope you'll catch them real soon."

Sam tossed a half-dollar into the waitress's tray. "Keep the change. And don't believe too much of what Henry Fossett puts in that paper of his. He can't explain what happened any better than we can. Blaming the Nazis as having a secret weapon is only hype to sell papers. Besides that, there aren't any Nazis here in Silver City."

Kathy turned to the sheriff, her voice was low when she said, "I wouldn't be so sure about that. Ed Von Gendren, the milkman, acts strange. He's up at all hours and acts like he has something to hide. I hear he also has family in Germany. It might be a good idea if you'd investigate him."

"Yes ma'am," Sam said sadly. "I will do just that."

After the waitress had left, Dr. Whitlock shook his head sadly. "They start so easily, these witch-hunts. Henry Fossett would have been right at home during the Inquisition. All it takes is to point out to average people that some among them are evil and need watching and it begins. Old women living alone with only a cat for company, a retarded man wandering about town, a neighbor who speaks with an accent. A little finger-pointing and they are all suspect, then become convicted in the court of imagination. This is going to get worse, Sam, a lot worse. Hate is the most contagious disease known to man."

"I'll have a chat with good ol' Henry Fossett in the morning.

Maybe I can convince him to settle down and quit stirring folks up until we get a handle on what's going on."

"Maybe it will rain, too."

"I intend to be *really* convincing. Every newspaper needs access to law enforcement. Hap Johnson, the town marshal, has gout so bad he can barely get around, so he's giving us most of his calls. If Fossett wants to keep in the know about what's going on in Grant County, he'd better play ball with us."

The coroner looked thoughtfully through a haze of cigarette smoke to a front window. "I really don't think Henry Fossett will pay any attention to you at all. His type ignores everyone who doesn't have the same rabid mind-set they do. Fossett is going to keep right on rousing the rabble by slanting the news any way he darn well pleases. The man's on a mission and the taco has slid off his Mexican plate."

Sam Sinrod cocked an eyebrow and drained the last golden drop from his bottle. "That would make for a bad combination."

Dr. Whitlock kept his thoughtful expression as he opened a fresh pack of Chesterfields and tapped one loose. "I find myself thinking that possibly this entire mess may just fade away. There's a world war raging and the country here's in a terrible drought. If no one else turns themselves into a pile of ash, people will begin to focus on other things and let us get back to solving normal murders and such."

"We can only hope that'll be the case." Sam smiled when he saw the lithe Kathy Webster approaching with a tray full of frosty brown bottles of Carling Black Label beer. "In any event, Archie's lounge is the best place I know of to wait and see what happens."

A couple of hours later a profusion of empty Carling Black Label beer bottles lined the wall side of Sinrod and Whitlock's booth. A blood-red half-moon could be seen through the window, hanging low in an inky sky.

"Well, Dr. Watson," Sam said. "I suppose I should go home and hit the sack. Tomorrow is shaping up to be a long day. And the game is afoot."

"Actually we have three you know." Whitlock noticed the look of puzzlement in his friend's face. "Feet that is. There are three of them over in the morgue."

"Yeah, I—"

A reflection of flashing red lights in the front windows along with the distant wailing of sirens took Sam Sinrod's attention as well as that of everyone else in Archie's lounge.

Dr. Whitlock saw Kathy Webster running toward them, her eyes again were wider than usual.

"There's been something terrible happen at Millie's. They need both of you there right away," Kathy shouted.

"Well, this is becoming repetitive," Sam grumbled as he joined the coroner in a dash for the door.

Chapter Nineteen

A fiery New Mexico sun was slowly sinking into a crimson pool over the Burro Mountains when Tasker Adams and Wesley Clinkenbeard came weaving their way up Little Walnut Creek. The Model A truck clipped a tree before chugging to a jerky stop midway between their house and garage. Both of the old men were thoroughly and delightfully drunk.

"I haven't felt this good since the last time we got stewed," Tasker said, attempting to find the door handle. After several minutes of fishing around he remembered it had fallen off over a year ago. He reached out the open window, turned the handle and nearly fell to the ground when the door opened. "Been a while, ain't it, pard?"

"It's been a while since we had a half sawbuck laid on us for a couple of hours' work," Wesley said, staggering to stand while keeping a bloody handkerchief plastered to his right ear. "I'm of the mind we shudda started drinking later in the morning."

"That would have kept a lot of folks at Dub's Place from having a good laugh when you went and shut your ear in the pickup's door. That's a feat few manage to accomplish."

"I ain't sure how that happened, but I fail to see the humor. The thing's still bleeding like a stuck hog, hurts like hell, too."

"Drinking beer since ten this morning is what caused it to happen, you old coot." Tasker gave a huge belch. "I'm of the mind that those shots of whiskey you added to the mix is the culprit that slammed your ear in the door. No wonder your tummy ain't up to snuff. Dub's bar whiskey comes out of Mexico. That rotgut's strong enough to burn a hole in an alligator's hide."

"How would you know, you never even seen an alligator in all of your born days."

"Tough things, those gators. I knew a gal up in Colorado once that had a purse made out of an alligator's hide. When she whacked you with that thing, you knew you'd been whacked, I'm here to tell you."

Wesley refolded the handkerchief and pressed it to his ear. "That was the school teacher if I recollect correctly. I always suspected she had good sense. Her name was Gertrude, which should have been a clue to head for tall timber even before you got her riled."

"She was a hot patootie in the sack, and I was in like Flynn. Women are just unpredictable critters. If her nosy sister hadn't seen me coming out of that cathouse, I'd likely be married today. Gertie had a dang good job, too. Be on easy street, I would, instead of putting up with the likes of you."

Wesley's ear was throbbing too much for any more reminiscing. "At least patching that hole wasn't as much work as we'd feared."

"Nope, it weren't. Those boards we had matched right up, which came as no great surprise. Putting in that new stringer was the worst part. Smells nastier than all get out in the basement."

"Having a prophet burn up down there is the likely cause. Be a long time before the stink's out. But on the good side, a body can't smell nothing bad while they're setting at the bar."

Tasker staggered around the Model A. "At least we made ourselves a half sawbuck. In hard times like these, that ain't nothing to sneeze at."

Wesley realized his ear had quit bleeding and shoved the

handkerchief into a pocket of his dirty overalls. "How much of that windfall do we have left after we went crazy?"

"Let me see." Tasker lumbered a few feet toward their front door to where a shaft of yellow moonlight was shooting through an opening in the enormous cottonwood trees that sheltered their clapboard cabin. After a few awkward attempts at counting he said, "My cipher gives us a dollar, two dimes and five pennies."

"You're saying we have a dollar and a quarter left out of a five-spot?"

"Nope, I'm telling you we have a silver dollar, two dimes and three pennies left out of the five bucks Dub paid us, added to the dollar and two nickels we left home with this morning."

"I thought you said we had five pennies."

"Can't see 'em now, must have been my eyes going a little bad on me." Tasker sighed. "I'm holding hopes we'll look back on this day with good feelings, considering it cost us seventy-five cents to patch a floor in a bar floor."

"No, it's seventy-eight cents, you old coot," Wesley grumbled. "You messed up on your cipher, again. No wonder Gertie whacked you with an alligator purse. You can be a real irritant to be around on occasion."

"It was your lame-brained idea to buy the bar a round. There went our profit, and it was none of my doing."

Wesley shook his head, which started his ear bleeding again. It took him a while to remember which pocket he had tucked the handkerchief into. "We're going to have to either become more frugal or start making more money."

Tasker gave another belch and wished that his partner hadn't wolfed down all of their baking soda. "I'm for making more money. Being economical ain't nearly as much fun. Besides that, we ain't old enough to start collecting any of President Roosevelt's rocking-chair money."

"We're old enough, you old codger. Both of us could get the old-age pension, but we got to sign up first."

"Maybe we could find someone who can read to help us fill out all those forms and get us through the paperwork," Tasker suggested.

"Then it'll take forever. I'm for opening up that thing we thought was a meteor and see what's inside. If it turns out to be quicksilver, we might make an entire sawbuck selling it to some gold mine."

"The gold mines are closed, remember. The government made a law only copper, lead, and zinc can be mined until the war's over."

"Well, damn if you ain't right for a change," Wesley said. "But it won't take a hard few minutes' work with a chisel to see what's inside. And I'm here to tell you not to get any of that green stuff on your skin, burns like hell for a few minutes."

"We'll get around to it. I need my sleep, drinking causes your skin to wrinkle otherwise, or so Gertie claimed."

Wesley snorted, "I can't say that theory will hold water. Take a gander in the mirror the next time you decide to shave."

The two old miners took several minutes trying to unlock the door before they realized they hadn't locked it in the first place. Once inside, Tasker began pumping the coffeepot full of water. Wesley turned on the Crosley radio, and sat down to wait for the coffee to perk while listening to a tune that was famous a couple of years ago. *I Don't Want to Set the World on Fire.*

Chapter Twenty

Madame Millie's stately mansion, affectionately dubbed "The Pussy Palace" by the male population because, no doubt, of a huge stone lion on each side of the entranceway, had long been a Silver City institution of basic pleasures.

The rambling, ornate Victorian structure sat on one of the few pieces of flat earth between highway 90 and a normally dry ravine that makes a long jagged gash through town, unimaginatively named "The Big Ditch." A young Billy the Kid lived near here for a while before his parents' house got washed away by a flash flood, giving impetus to his moving on to Lincoln County and fame.

On a normal night, only a solitary red globe shining over the doorway illuminated the outside of Millie's mansion, no other type of advertising being necessary. Tonight, however, the parking lot and highway in front was awash with flashing red lights from emergency vehicles of every description. Shadows danced eerily among enormous cottonwood trees and reflected from the rocky chasm behind the huge two-story frame house.

"I sure hope this turns out to be just a simple case of murder," Sam Sinrod said as he skidded the cruiser to a dusty stop behind Freeman Bates' GMC pickup. "Or at least a crime that you can find in a law book."

"This much is certain, my dear Sherlock," the coroner said as he pulled the door handle. "We're going to find out real shortly."

The fire chief came ambling toward them, puffing on a pipe.

"We got lucky on this one. Only a mattress and part of a floor burnt before we put the fire out. It would be a terrible tragedy for the entire southwest if Madame Millie's joint went up in smoke." Freeman Bates turned and stared at the mansion, his grim features framed by shimmering beams of red lights. "The girl's front got scorched, but I don't think she's burned too bad. To be on the safe side, considering the circumstances, I sent her to the hospital to get checked over. All that's left of the man is most of one leg and a foot, the rest of him is nothing but ashes."

Sheriff Sinrod growled, "*Another* man went up in flames and you're just getting to the point. And how did this girl come to get burned?"

Freeman coughed slightly. "She was sorta underneath him when he lit off and went up in flames like Joan of Arc. Hell's bells, Sam, you do know what goes on here, I hope."

"This sounds like another one for the record books," Dr. Whitlock said taking a leather-covered notebook and pen from his shirt pocket. "Maybe the lady can tell us something that might give us some kind of clue, like what the poor guy ate or drank. I'll go check on her when we're done here. Who was the man, by the way, does anyone know?"

The fire chief took a moment to tamp the tobacco firm in his pipe and relight it. "You guys are simply gonna love this part. His clothes, of course, weren't on him at the time so they never even got singed. We have his wallet *and* his badge. Turns out the man's name was Roan Walker. It seems he was the chief arson investigator for the state boys." Freeman clucked his tongue. "I'd say the entire matter's a tad ironic: an arson investigator comes to Silver City, catches fire for no good reason and comes dang near to burning down a first-class cathouse."

"I'd say Doc's right about this being one for the books," Sam Sinrod said with a sigh. "I'll fetch the camera and flash attachment, take some pictures then scoop up anything that looks like human remains," he nodded to Bryce. "Why don't you go see to the girl, find out what she knows. I'll come by the morgue when I'm done. This is going to be another long night. Now with a policeman killed, we had better start boilerplating our butts with paperwork."

"I agree," Freeman Bates said. "I doubt there'll be enough rooms at the hotel to hold all the police that'll be showing up from the capital. And every single one of those pencil pushers is going to want to go over paperwork. I'd say we'd best oblige them, even if we don't know anything."

A dusky-skinned, raven-haired young woman lying on a narrow hospital bed beneath an open window turned her head to face Dr. Whitlock when he came into the room. Scores of moths crashed and fluttered against the screen, making a pinging sound akin to raindrops.

"I'm a doctor and the county medical investigator, miss," Dr. Whitlock said soothingly. "Do you speak English?"

"My name is Rosemaria Bettencourt, Doc. My parents were French but I was born in New Orleans. To answer your question, I speak both French and English quite fluently. Now it's your turn to answer me a question."

Bryce Whitlock stepped alongside the bed. He could not help but admire the voluptuous form covered only by a single white sheet. The woman seemed to be more irate than hurt. Sparks of anger flickered in anthracite eyes that were charmingly enhanced by layers of jade-colored eye shadow. He took note of bee-stung lips painted bright crimson along with thickly rouged cheeks and long scarlet-colored fingernails.

Dr. Whitlock thought that possibly Rosemaria had taken the term "painted lady" a bit too seriously. Upon closer examination, he decided the woman was considerably older than she wished anyone to know. It was more than possible Rosemaria could be well into her thirties, an old age for girls who worked at Madame Millie's place.

"Ask away," Whitlock said eventually.

"What, in the name of hell, *happened* to that man! Doc, I've been making my living on my back for over twenty years. I have known thousands of different men, but having a john catch on fire during a poke is something I've never even heard of. And us girls run across a lot of really weird stuff."

Dr. Whitlock swallowed. He was not accustomed to hearing such crude talk, especially from the fair sex. "Ma'am, Miss Bettencourt, I am going to tell you the truth. No one has any idea why not only that man, but three others have suddenly burst into flames. It might be helpful if you could tell me what he drank, or if you can recall anything out of the ordinary occurring."

"Listen, Doc," Rosemaria flipped the sheet from her naked body. "Take a gander at what that freak did to me. I'm so scorched I'll be out of business for days. That'll cost me a lot of money. Anyway, I was doing what I get paid for, when all of a sudden this guy feels real hot, then his eyes get all buggy and glazed over, like maybe he's having a heart attack. I wiggled out quick as I could, but not quick enough . . . he was fat, you know. Then the jerk simply started sizzling and burning like he was made out of pitch."

Dr. Whitlock took a careful study of the reddened flesh that covered the front of her body. "First-degree burns is all they are; I'll order some lotion and have the nurse give you a mild sedative. You are a lucky lady. Roan Walker completely burned through the mattress and halfway through the floor. It could have been much worse."

"So that was the creep's name. I never ask, or care." Rosemaria pulled the sheet up to cover her naked body. "Listen,

Doc, you may think these burns are nothing, but they hurt like hell. I don't know a single reason why that bastard or any of those other guys burnt up and I don't give a rat's ass. Just as soon as I'm able, I'm leaving this one-horse burg and going back to New Orleans where men have the decency not to catch fire while making love to a woman."

Dr. Whitlock simply nodded.

"I'm in pain, Doc," Rosemaria's voice turned pleading. "Could you give me, you know, some *good* stuff? I really need it. A nice big dose of morphine will let me get some sleep."

"I'll order you a shot," Bryce Whitlock turned and strode out without saying another word. This fallen angel was so hardened by life and beset by her own demons that it would be a waste of time to ask her to help fight another.

Dr. Whitlock moved a handheld magnifying glass back and forth to focus on the charred stump of leg lying on the stainless-steel autopsy table. "I must say, Sam, this is the most we've had to work with, so far."

"We aim to please." Sam Sinrod lit a cigar. "Too bad the girl wasn't any help."

"Life has hardened her while squeezing out every iota of compassion. I find that sad." The coroner's eyebrows drew together in concentration. "What the heck?"

"Did you find something?"

"Possibly, quite possibly. There are dark jagged lines radiating outward from the femur bone. They look just like little bolts of black lightning. I'm wondering if something electrical could be causing this to happen. Maybe Roan's leg here became grounded on a bedspring or something that stopped the process of combustion."

The sheriff blew a smoke ring and watched it drift to the ceiling. "Not soon enough that it did him any good."

"No, but if it is electrical, we have a whole new avenue to explore and can look for causes."

"Percy Guttman was miles out of town in a field when he fired off. There were no power lines close and there hasn't been any storm let alone an electrical storm for weeks. How can we begin to explain him coming into contact with any current? Then we have the Prophet, who was in a bar drinking beer. If beer was the cause, we'd both be toast."

Dr. Whitlock sighed, placed the magnifying glass aside, draped a sheet over the remains and reached for a pack of Chesterfields. "I think the electricity theory needs some study before we go bandying it about." He nodded to the autopsy table. "You notify Santa Fe?"

"I did," Sam said. "I told them that Officer Walker was taking a water sample in a house when he met with an unexplained accident. For all we know the fellow has a wife and kids. They don't need to learn more than they have to."

"That was decent of you. I can't see where it'll change anything important to the facts."

"Yeah, that's my feelings." Sam stepped over to the counter and flicked an ash from his cigar into the sink. "Speaking of facts, we're both going to be in for a lot more affliction once word of what we did gets out."

The corner's brow furrowed in puzzlement. "What *we* did."

"There's no way to deny it, either." Sam Sinrod's voice grew serious. "We were in a bar, fiddling around while Roan burned."

Chapter Twenty-One

The print room of the *Silver City Times* was always quiet as the inside of a tomb during the wee hours of morning, which, in the mind of Henry Fossett, made for perfect concentration of the senses.

The scarecrow-like editor sat on a three-legged stool in front of the massive Linotype machine that he alone had control over. The power of truth was inside of the device, if only he could use his skilled hands to print the words of warning to people who understood the dangers of procrastination. He smoked a crooked cigar while flexing his spindly fingers. A cold hangman's smile lay emotionless on his cadaverous face that was illuminated by a shaft of yellow moonlight. There was simply so much truth . . . needed truth . . . to be printed that his mind was awash with reality.

It maddened Henry Fossett that he alone must shoulder the burden of removing fascism from the confines of Silver City. The sheriff was a dolt, going to him with the truth would be a total waste of his valuable time. The other newspapers to which he had sent previous copies of his wake-up call about sedition being rampant, had completely ignored his entreaties. The tentacles of Naziism were far more tortuous and intertwined than even he had realized. It was shocking to find that such a prestigious and formerly stalwart newspaper as the *New York Times* had come under control of one of Adolf Hitler's minions.

But that was the only explanation for them ignoring his repeated entreaties.

Henry Fossett reminded himself to not be unduly harsh on the average citizen. The enemy was quite talented, and they had been perfecting their grip on the minds of innocent, trusting souls for many long years. Their seductive, treacherous intentions were as invisible as plague germs. And just as deadly.

He decided with a surge of resolution there was no time left for mollycoddling softheaded idiots who were afraid to take a stand to defend their homeland. No, Henry Fossett affirmed, he had already wasted far too much precious time withholding truth. The people, the innocent God-fearing people of Grant County, would surely heed his call to arms when they read about how infested with Nazis the government had become.

The melodic, soothing voice of Saint John the Divine spoke inside of his head, telling him to proceed, that he was doing God's Will.

Then, a new voice unfamiliar to him began orating with such sweet power that Henry became afraid the words could be overheard. He smiled at the thought that his spirit guides would allow such a dastardly thing to happen, the words were for him alone. Henry Fossett bolted upright when the new voice identified itself. Jesus Christ himself had heard his pleas! Saint John joined our Lord and Savior in urging him to print the truth. Now! These were the words he had been awaiting for such a long time.

It was time to open the floodgates of light upon the dark, insidious demons of evil and cause them, along with their blight, to be removed from the face of God's good earth.

Cheered on by voices only he could hear, Henry Fossett leaned back on the oak stool and placed his dainty fingers on the keyboard. His focus was so intent he did not notice a shadow moving among shadows in the dark room. Nor did he hear the soft falling of leather shoes on concrete. Henry Fossett did, however, hear the whistling of a crowbar as it sliced through the still night air on its mission to shatter his skull.

But by then it did not matter.

Chapter Twenty-Two

Payatt Hae was not surprised to find that the eyes of *Usen* were red. He was, however, taken aback that there were so *many* of them.

To summon and help the great Earth god in his task of destroying the hated *Pinda-lik-o-yi*'s windmill, the venerable old Apache wore a colorful headdress made of feathers from a bald eagle. In all of nature no other creature had such wonderful eyesight. A bald eagle could spot a fish swimming deep in murky water or a snake slithering among shadows. With such wonderful assistance as an eagle's vision, the Great *Usen* would surely not miss with his next fireball. After the windmill had been flattened his spring would flow life-giving water once again. Then he could stop paying good money for water, which the gods meant to be free to all of The People.

A wan moon hanging in a jeweled canopy of satin night gave Payatt ample light to study *Usen*'s strange movements on the distant cliffs. It appeared that *Usen* was only looking the windmill over with dozens of fiery eyes. This was not what Payatt Hae had expected would be the case. Any god worth his salt should realize that another huge fireball was what was needed to smash a windmill. Simply looking it over was a waste of time.

For a long while Payatt Hae stood in the night and watched the many red eyes of *Usen* flit about the distant mountainside like fireflies. Then to his dismay the lights vanished. A moment later came a growl that reminded him of a provoked bear. Then there was only the stone silence of night in the desert.

The ways of the gods are not for man to understand. Payatt Hae knew that he must accept *Usen*'s judgment, no matter how much it puzzled and exasperated him. The hated *Pinda-lik-o-yi*'s windmill would stay as it was. Perhaps, Payatt mused, the white man's one God could have had a visit with *Usen* and persuaded him to not destroy the windmill for some reason. When gods get together, often they become tired from too much talk and go to sleep. It was also quite possible that all of those eyes did not belong to the Earth god. That would explain much.

No matter. It was late. The old Apache sadly took off the wonderful headdress of eagle feathers, tucked it safely under his arm and began the trek home. He brightened when he thought of the steaming cup of hot chocolate that Chepi would have ready when he arrived. Of all of the gifts and wonders of the white man, none were better than hot chocolate.

Tomorrow he would drive to Silver City and buy more water. Payatt thought he might try beseeching other gods to help flatten that windmill. The white men had only one god, who could not possibly be everywhere all of the time. The Apache did not suffer such a handicap, they had many gods to rely on. And at least some of them had to be awake. But for tonight however, Payatt Hae had his home, his wife and hot chocolate. A man should never ask for too much, too soon.

CHAPTER TWENTY-THREE

Another day was being born hot and dry on a bloody horizon when Sam Sinrod turned the cruiser into his private parking space alongside the sheriff's department. He was forced to slam on the brakes to keep from crashing into the rear of a huge, black, 1936 Packard Super Eight that filled the slot.

"Cripes," Sam grumbled when he recognized the car, "of all of the birds to come waddling down from Santa Fe, why did it have to be those two goons?"

Lieutenant Neto Diego and the sinister Sergeant Garret Black were both state troopers who had been to Silver City before to cause him, along with everyone else, grief. While the duo sported uniforms and badges that announced them to be state troopers, Sam knew better. They were hired killers who worked directly for Governor Castle and Attorney General Jack Sutton. Nicknamed "the Janitors" by those in the know, Diego and Black cleaned up potential political messes using direct, usually lethal means. In a nutshell, they where hired killers. But why those creeps had come to Silver City was a mystery. As far as Sam Sinrod knew there was no way professional hit men could stop people from catching fire if they were of a mind to do so.

The sheriff remembered that hugely fat Lieutenant Diego hated cigar smoke worse than anything. He tarried long enough to fish a long black Cuban from his shirt pocket and fire it before striding up the stairs to his office.

Deputy Burke Martin was at the reception desk. He looked relieved to see him. "Sheriff, there's two state—"

"I know, Burke," Sam said. He coughed to disguise a sigh. "I have already noticed the gentlemen's car parked in my space. I'll handle the matter."

The door had not completed its opening arc before Neto Diego grumbled, "Sheriff Sinrod, we have been waiting for a *very* long time."

Sam smiled socially as he walked over and shook the hands of the two officers who remained seated. He plopped into the oak chair behind his desk and slouched. "Being a hick sheriff in a county full of apple-knockers means I can stay in the sack clear 'til late in the morning." He motioned to the Regulator clock on the wall. "Shucks it's only seven, reckon I could've taken time to shave."

"And we," Neto Diego grinned at the sheriff with the cold expression of a cat staring at a goldfish, "are *most* happy to be here working with you again. I am certain we will get along fabulously."

"Shit-kicking town," Garret Black said.

Sam Sinrod eyed the beanpole-thin sergeant and decided he had lost weight since their last encounter. The six-foot-tall Garret Black now likely only weighed one hundred and thirty pounds at most. *Being forced to subsist on raw eggs after having most of your stomach blown away by a shotgun blast could account for the loss,* Sam thought.

The sheriff forced a thin smile. "Good to see you again too, Sergeant Black." He took a long puff on his cigar before turning to the rotund lieutenant who had put on more weight than Garret had lost. Almost certainly the state trooper would be forced to go to a feed store to find scales that would register high enough to indicate his bulk. Neto Diego had to be at least three hundred pounds.

"I'm sorry about what happened to Officer Walker," Sam said from a cloud of cigar smoke.

The chair groaned ominously as the fat lieutenant attempted to scoot away from Sam's cigar. "We are planning to meet him for breakfast." Neto's expression turned puzzled as he said hesitantly, "Has something happened here that we are not aware of?"

Sheriff Sinrod cocked his head in amazement. "Roan Walker's left leg is all that we recovered after he caught fire and burned up over in Madame Millie's cathouse last night."

Neto and Garret exchanged glances of genuine surprise.

"This is the first we've heard of it," Neto complained.

"It's a long drive down here," Sergeant Black grumbled. "The roads are bad and we're busy men. The two of us only call into Santa Fe when we need to. Normally, the lieutenant and I handle matters on our own."

Neto Diego blinked watery eyes. "May I ask how and exactly when this unfortunate event occurred?"

Sam Sinrod's brow furrowed. "Ah, uh, he was—sampling at the time. Water that is. Last night, yeah. It was only about eight o'clock. Officer Walker was taking a water sample when he just caught on fire and burned up."

"I told you this was a shit-kicking town," Garret Black growled. "Strange things like this only happen in shit-kicking towns."

The sheriff never had time to utter another word before Deputy Martin swung open the door and yelled, "There's been a murder at the newspaper. Henry Fossett's been killed! Dr. Whitlock's already at the scene."

"Since we are already here, we will be most happy to assist in the investigation," Neto Diego said with a grunt as he forced his bulk to stand. "There are already enough unsolved murders hereabouts for you to investigate, Sheriff Sinrod."

"Shit-kicking town," Garret Black mumbled as he joined the exodus to the newspaper office.

CHAPTER TWENTY-FOUR

Dr. Bryce Whitlock stood on the sidewalk outside the open front door of the *Silver City Times.* He sighed when he noticed the familiar black Packard Super Eight pull to a stop behind the sheriff's cruiser. The way things had been going lately, Diego and Black's appearance came as no great surprise. He consoled himself with the thought that if those two hired killers were to catch on fire, he wouldn't consider the event to be a loss. Marshmallows and hot dogs would certainly be in order.

Neil Halfman, one of Sam Sinrod's deputies, sprinted toward the arriving lawmen. "I think, Sheriff, it'd be a good idea to put out that cigar. Most of the gas has probably aired out by now, but I'd hate to be mistaken and blow up our only newspaper building."

"What do you mean about gas?" Sam asked, snubbing out the fire and tucking his cigar into the ashtray before climbing out of the cruiser.

The deputy nodded to an ashen-faced older man who stood shivering alongside the coroner in spite of the building heat. "John Curtis over there's the printer. When he came to work this morning, he smelled gas. He opened all the doors and windows, then found someone had unscrewed the gas line to the heater. That was when he saw the body."

Neto Diego and Garret Black shoved the sheriff aside as they charged the front door.

"We are here to take charge of this investigation," Neto

growled at the coroner when he stepped to block their entry to the sprawling brick building.

Dr. Whitlock placed an obviously forced smile on his face. "Since the murder occurred in Grant County and I am the coroner, I think that a more homogeneous approach would pay dividends."

Garret Black instinctively placed a hand on his pistol as he spun to the lieutenant and growled, "Did that son of a bitch just call us what I think he did?"

Lieutenant Diego shook his head. "The good doctor simply made a rather wordy suggestion that we should all cooperate in this investigation." He sighed resignedly. "Sadly I am forced to concur."

"One big happy family of lawmen out to catch a killer," Sam Sinrod said. "What a novel idea. Now let's go look at the scene of the crime."

The body of Henry Fossett lay sprawled face-up alongside an overturned chair in front of the Linotype machine. A circular pool of blood was thick on the concrete floor beneath his head. A horde of green flies were happily at work lapping away at the crimson feast.

Dr. Whitlock bent over and touched Fossett's jaw, sending a cloud of flies buzzing. "He's been dead for at least a few hours. Rigor mortis is just now beginning to set in. My best guess is that death occurred between two and three this morning."

"There's no guessing at what killed him," Sam Sinrod pointed to a long steel crowbar laying a few feet away. "Our esteemed editor never felt any pain, that's for sure. The whole back of his head is smashed in like it was a ripe melon."

Sergeant Black reached down and picked up the crowbar. "Yep, this is the murder weapon all right. There's dried blood and bits of flesh and hair on it."

Sam Sinrod gnashed his teeth. "If there were any fingerprints on that crowbar, you just destroyed them."

"I don't hold with any of that modern stuff, Sheriff Sinrod." Black handed him the crowbar. "In my experience I've found that a really good pistol whipping generally gets me all of the information I need."

"Whoever the killer was, he actually intended to blow the whole building up to cover his tracks," Neil Halfman interjected from over by the far wall. "That's why he turned the gas on after taking the pipe loose from the wall. And come look at the rest of the plan."

The lawmen came over to where the deputy was pointing to a partially melted candle sitting on the end of a workbench underneath a high window.

"Gas is heavier than air, so it stays low on the floor. When it built up heavy enough, the candle was to ignite it," Neil said. "It would have worked too, if this big moth hadn't knocked out the flame."

The coroner pulled a singed, dead moth loose from a pool of hardened wax at the base of the candle. "It's from the order *Lepidoptera,* a sphinx moth. I'm betting this insect saved most of the town from burning. If this building had exploded, dry as it is, fire would have scattered all over."

"Then build a monument to it," Garret Black spat. "The lieutenant and I are going to check into the Copper Mountain Hotel and have an early lunch. You boys seem to want to handle this, so handle away."

After the state lawmen had climbed into their huge black Packard and driven off, Sam, Neil and the coroner stood looking at the body.

"For being in such a hurry to take charge of this investigation they sure took off in a hurry," Neil Halfman said. "That's really strange."

"All those two goons wanted to do was to be here long

enough to cover their own mistakes. They hadn't planned on that moth stopping the explosion and fire they'd counted on. What they wanted to do was make certain there was nothing to connect Fossett's murder to them."

"But those men are state troopers," Neil said. "Not killers."

"Oh, they work for the state," Bryce Whitlock said. "Calling them lawmen, however, is a really long reach."

"Sergeant Black picking up that crowbar was to have a reason for his prints being on it." Sam stared at Henry Fossett's remains. "That man made a lot of enemies with his poison pen. I'd expect more than a few of them must have been politicians."

Deputy Halfman shook his head in disbelief. "I still have a hard time believing that any of our state policemen would come in and simply kill a man to silence him."

"Think about it for a minute," Sam said. "Diego and Black said they were here to help us investigate a murder. Did you ever hear them once ask who the victim was?"

The deputy's mouth dropped open. "They knew!" he exclaimed.

Dr. Whitlock placed a hand on Neil's shoulder. "Go over to Barth Thornton's and tell the undertaker to bring the hearse straightway. I want to get Fossett moved to a cooler climate before he gets gamey. Later I'll have to do an autopsy, but what bothers me is this case has nothing to do with why those other folks caught on fire."

Neil Halfman looked at the dead sphinx moth that was still in the coroner's other hand. "And a common moth is all that saved Silver City from burning down."

"Yeah," Sam Sinrod said, turning to leave. "We're really good at protecting our citizens."

A distant boom took everyone's attention.

"Now that was an explosion if I've ever heard one," Neil Halfman said excitedly.

The men ran outside to where a column of black smoke could be seen rising in the distance.

"That's coming from up on Little Walnut Creek," the deputy said turning to the sheriff. "Right near where your house is, or I miss my guess."

Chapter Twenty-Five

"We're going to have to buy some more coffee." Wesley Clinkenbeard tapped the metal can he held over the open pot to shake loose any contents that remained. "After what happened to us yesterday, suffering through a morning with weak coffee's an agony to endure."

"You're the idiot that bought the bar a round then started me to drinking some of Dub's rotgut whiskey." Tasker Adams went to the kitchen cabinet, opened a bottom door that was hung with only one hinge. He stood, grinned and handed his friend a three-pound unopened can of Folgers coffee. "And now your memory has gone to pot. I swear, if it wasn't for me taking care of business, you'd starve to death under a tree somewhere."

"Well, I plumb forgot about that coffee," Wesley grabbed an opener from a drawer and began to crank it around the can of hangover cure they both needed desperately. "It would have gone bad before Otis gets back from the war anyway."

"Yeah," Tasker agreed. "And there's no incentive to spend time in a cabin that's got no floor. Been a waste to have just gone off and left it there."

"Frugal, that's what we are." Wesley spooned some coffee into the pot then set it on the already glowing hot plate. "Folks just plain don't take care of their possessions these days, leaving stuff laying around to spoil or rust away like they do."

"You're right there, pard. It's a sad trait to see developing in mankind. I reckon you could say we're doing our best to teach folks to be more responsible in looking after their things."

"And we're doing it for free, too."

Tasker Adams rubbed a shaky hand through his silver hair and glared at the chipped porcelain coffeepot. "Dang water takes forever to boil up here in the high country. I'm of the mind we ought to stop by the store and buy some of that G. Washington's instant coffee. Be a godsend to have a can of that stuck back for mornings like this one."

"There won't be many of these to suffer through if we don't get our hands on some more money right soon. Silver City's fresh out of prophets to help us get floor-patching jobs."

"I'm saying we have a solid six tons of scrap iron to sell Lonnie Dillman. Factor in those ten cases of DuPont dynamite that'll fetch us at least three bucks a box and we'll be in fine shape for a spell."

Wesley blinked and cocked his head. "I thought we had figured on getting five bucks a case for that dynamite."

"I'm afraid a few of those boxes might be a tad too fuzzy to fetch a premium price. Some people are downright skittish about using sticks of powder covered with nitroglycerine crystals all over 'em."

"Can't say I blame them none. Might be a good idea to make that mine over in Fiero an even better deal if they'll come and haul it way themselves. I don't fancy getting blown to smithereens, especially when we know better."

"I swear," Tasker said, "you *are* becoming a Caspar Milquetoast. It takes a hard whack to set off even old dynamite. And we ain't going to mistreat it any."

Wesley gave a satisfied look at the coffeepot that had just begun to perk. "Well, we have to find someone willing to buy it before getting too concerned. The scrap iron is a sure thing."

"Don't forget we've still got that blamed military canister to chisel open. Gold mines or no gold mines operating, I heard folks talking in Dub's that quicksilver is bringing three dollars a pound."

"While we're on the subject of people talking," Wesley said with concern, "there's been other folks besides the Prophet deciding to burn up. I heard a banjo player in a medicine show caught fire and blew up a truck."

"Never can trust banjo players or fiddlers. They'll steal the fillings outta your teeth." Tasker's eyebrows drew down in thought. "Maybe someone else will go and burn another hole through Dub's floor. We still have plenty of oak planking left."

Wesley shook his head sadly and rubbed the bandage on his ear. "I reckon it is best to be an optimist." He nodded to the coffeepot. "Let's have a cup or two of java and then go see what's inside that Army thing."

The sun was high and blazing bright in a cloudless blue sky before Tasker and Wesley felt up to venturing out of the comfort of their small home. One of the benefits of living beneath a thicket of cottonwood trees was having shade most of the day. This had been a summer where the advantageous location nearly outweighed being neighbors to the county sheriff.

"I sure wish you hadn't swallowed all of our baking soda," Tasker complained as they headed to the garage doors. "Bad whiskey is playing hob with my innards."

"No one held a gun to your head to make you drink it," Wesley said, looking to Sam Sinrod's house. "Actually, I think Dub's whiskey tastes plenty good. It was those thirty odd glasses of beer that's causing your problems. Next time I'd stop at twenty if I were you."

Tasker Adams joined his friend in scanning the sheriff's place.

"Reckon we can get on with our work," Wesley said, grabbing onto one of the garage door handles. "If we don't get some more boodle you might be forced to get healthy."

"What the hell is that sound?" Tasker asked as he opened the door. "Look at that, it's a big rat," Wesley said, "and it's running around in circles squealing and smoking."

"Never seen a rat smoking before."

"Strange summer this one is," Tasker said, then backed up a step. "I swear that rat's starting to shoot off sparks. They shouldn't do that."

"Not in here," Wesley yelled in alarm. "Not with ten cases of DuPont dynamite along with a few boxes of blasting caps to keep it company."

The two old miners gave each other a wide-eyed glance then ran and jumped into their Model A truck. They had just made it past Sam Sinrod's house before a ball of fire filled the canyon followed by a tremendous explosion that ripped the still, hot air with the force of a huge bomb.

Chapter Twenty-Six

The harried waitress in the restaurant of the Copper Mountain Hotel could not help but stare when the skinny Sergeant Black took the six raw eggs he had ordered and began breaking them into a tall glass. He amazed her even further by adding a half bottle of hot pepper sauce along with a shot of whiskey to the ghastly mix and begin sipping it with obvious relish. The obnoxious fat officer who sat across from the pasty-faced egg sucker was slicing into the biggest porterhouse steak the cook could find. Surrounding the steak platter was most of everything on the menu, including an entire chocolate cake.

To add to her woes, the two uniformed state policemen seemed to be in an especially foul mood and were obviously arguing with each other. If those two gumshoes didn't leave a good tip after all of her hard work to please them, this would definitely have been a really great day to call in sick.

"How was I supposed to know some damn bug would fly into that candle and put the fire out," Garret Black grumbled to Neto after taking another sip of raw egg. "It would never happen again in a thousand years."

"It was *your* job to think of such things, Sergeant, you are a professional. Now we have a dead body laying around that we hadn't counted on. A really big explosion and fire was what we needed. The entire affair was supposed to look like an accident. The mark would simply have appeared to have been an unfortunate victim of a terrible explosion that destroyed much of the town. Considering how much you like Silver City, I expected you to be more diligent. You should have used more candles."

"I didn't want the place to look like a Mexican funeral parlor, for cripes sake."

Neto Diego glowered ominously.

"Sorry," Garret said quickly. "Just a figure of speech. On the good side the mark is whacked and if that hick sheriff pokes his nose where he shouldn't, I'll whack him too. And I'll do it for free; I don't like that man at all."

"I think Sheriff Sinrod has more important things to concern him than the death of Henry Fossett. When I phoned Santa Fe before we went to lunch, we were instructed to assist in the investigation of people catching on fire here in Silver City."

"You are referring to those cases of spontaneous human combustion like what happened to the junk dealer, Krook, in Charles Dickens' novel *Bleak House.*"

Neto Diego's expression turned blank. "Huh?"

Garret Black shrugged. "You should read more good books. Lieutenant, in spontaneous human combustion people just burn up for no reason, no gasoline or anything. I've looked into it quite a lot. In our line of work, being able to cause people to turn into a pile of ash without leaving anything to trace them back to us would be simply wonderful."

"I see your point, Sergeant, but are you telling me no one knows what causes those people to catch on fire?"

"Nope, not a clue. And scientists have been looking into it for years. Personally, I think it must be some chemical in the water. The sheriff did say Officer Walker was sampling some when he lit off."

"If no one has any idea what causes this spontaneous human combustion, then our bosses can't expect us to solve anything. You know, I like this hotel. The food is quite passable and we have not had a vacation for some time. We have a generous expense account. I suggest we relax and enjoy our stay here."

"These *are* good eggs," Garret Black agreed with a sinister smirk. "Besides, I've got a gut feeling I'm gonna have to whack that sheriff. If we stick around for a while it'll save us another trip."

"See," Neto said, sliding the chocolate cake close. "Every cloud has a silver lining if one only takes the time to look for it."

Chapter Twenty-Seven

"I'm plenty sorry about this," Fire Chief Freeman Bates said to Sam Sinrod as they surveyed the damage to his house. "But I'd say having just a couple of windows blown out as getting off easy, compared to how big that blast was. It's also a miracle no fires got started, dry as it is."

The sheriff poked his head through a shattered window. Jasper could be seen sleeping on the sofa, causing Sam to wonder anew about his cat's mental functions. A smart dog would still be running after the explosion that had been strong enough to rattle windows all the way down in Silver City.

Dr. Whitlock placed a comforting hand on Sam's shoulder. "Things like this are considered odd in most towns. I would say we are really fortunate not to have to deal with boredom living here in such a delightful town."

The sheriff looked up the canyon to where only a few broken stumps remained of what had been some of the biggest trees in Grant County. Where his neighbor's home used to be was now a section of mountainside the size of a football field, that had been scoured to bare rock.

"What in the name of everything holy did those old geezers have up there to blow up like that?" Freeman Bates asked.

Sam Sinrod clucked his tongue. "Tasker Adams and Wesley Clinkenbeard are scroungers. I've known for some time about them pilfering scrap iron from the mines. We need that for the war effort so I've let them go. Then, I had a call from a rancher up near Pinos Altos that they were hauling old dynamite out of a mine tunnel there. I assume that's what caused the explosion."

"No it wasn't," Tasker Adams poked a cautious face around the corner of the sheriff's house. "A rat's what caused the accident, a great big burning rat, shooting off sparks, it was, Wesley and me's darn lucky to have made it down the road before the explosion. Close call, that was."

The sheriff blinked in surprise. "I thought we'd be picking what was left of you two out of trees."

"Ain't no trees anymore," Wesley said, accompanying his partner to visit the sheriff. Both of the old miners were still too dazed to worry about going to jail. "That blast pretty much wrecked them."

"What's this nonsense about a rat?" Sam Sinrod asked testily. "And just how much dynamite did you two idiots have stashed up there, for Pete's sake?"

"Ten cases was all," Tasker Adams answered meekly. "Just ten."

"The rat's what caused it all," Wesley Clinkenbeard said. "You really had to be there to understand. That rat caught on fire like the Prophet that burnt up in Dub's Place. It was squealing something fierce, smoking like a chimney."

Tasker cocked his head and thought, *It's time to watch what I say here.* "My pard and me figured that dynamite would be a danger to any kids who might run across it. We took it on ourselves to keep them safe, so we hauled it here planning to give it to a mine. Help out with the war effort, you know."

Sam Sinrod rolled his eyes. Those two old men could stack it higher and deeper than anyone he had ever run across. He reminded himself that he had insurance to replace his shattered windows. His neighbors had lost everything. Even if they were hauling off everything in Grant County not nailed down with really big nails, they were now homeless.

Dr. Whitlock's thoughts were the same as the sheriff's. "I don't suppose you fellows had any insurance," the coroner asked knowing what the answer would be.

"Never needed any before now," Tasker Adams said honestly.

Wesley stared up the canyon. "It's kind of scattered around, but I think we can recover most of the scrap iron. Might get us thirty dollars or so."

"Cost us more than that to put up even a shack," Tasker Adams said sadly. "Reckon we're finally busted, pard. And all because of an overheated rat, beats all I ever seen."

Freeman Bates had overheard the conversation. "You two are on the old-age pension aren't you? Rooms in town aren't too expensive."

"We've been planning on doing that," Wesley said. "But there's lots of paperwork to deal with."

The fire chief realized the old men couldn't read. "Come by the station tomorrow, I'll have the forms and help you fill them out." He hesitated. "Government paperwork isn't an easy thing."

"Thanks, Chief," Tasker said. "I reckon we can sleep in the back of our truck, ain't likely to rain or nothing. My pard and me's only got a dollar and a quarter to our name."

"A dollar, two dimes and three pennies," Wesley corrected. "The old codger can't cipher worth a hoot."

Sam Sinrod felt a burning in his throat. That was always a sure sign he was planning to do something stupid. The two reprobates had been stealing anything they could sell, they had nearly wrecked his house and set fire to the countryside, yet the sheriff felt terribly sorry for them. Being broke and old was a sad situation.

"The county wound up with Dora Malone's house out in Chloride Flats for taxes. After she passed away, there wasn't any family to be found." Freeman Bates surprised everyone with his idea. "The treasurer has it up for tax sale, I think forty dollars will buy it. Shucks, the house has all the furniture, cookstove and everything still in it, be a right good place to live."

And the location is a nice safe distance from my house, Sam Sinrod thought. "Sounds like you fellows couldn't go wrong on a deal like that."

Tasker worried his lower lip. "Nope, if we had the forty bucks, we'd move right in. But we ain't, and I can't say we're likely to ever see such a windfall. Wesley's back's busted up and I'm so old no one will hire me."

Dr. Whitlock and Sam exchanged knowing glances.

"I'll loan you fellows twenty-five bucks," the sheriff said.

"And you can count me in for the same," Dr. Whitlock added, fishing for his wallet.

"This is not gift," Sam Sinrod said firmly. "When you fellows start collecting your pension, which will be a least twenty dollars a month, each, we expect to be paid back at five dollars a month."

"You can depend on us," Wesley Clinkenbeard said, his mouth hanging open from the unexpected turn of fortune. "Tasker and me are trustworthy as a preacher."

Sam Sinrod sighed as he handed over the cash. "You fellows go straight to town and buy that house. I don't want you to disappoint us on this. Making a sheriff angry isn't a smart thing to do."

"Yes sir," Tasker Adams agreed. "We'll even vote for you this time around, didn't do that the last election."

The sheriff and Dr. Whitlock watched as Freeman Bates' fire truck followed the old men's Model A down the canyon.

"We'll never see a dime back," Sam said.

"I'm betting we will," Dr. Whitlock said, his features tight with thought. "They're basically honest enough. I keep thinking on that rat they claimed was on fire. It is possible whatever's causing spontaneous human combustion in people might also affect animals. We simply don't know, but I'm thinking they might be telling the truth there."

"Wonderful, simply wonderful. Now we have burning rats to deal with, as if there wasn't enough to worry over before." Sam kicked a piece of broken glass with his boot. "Well, Dr. Watson, let's go back and take care of a murder. This is shaping up to be another long, hard day. I'll send Burke Martin out to cover the holes with some boards I've got in the shed until I can get some new glass put in."

"We've not done too bad," Tasker Adams said as he and his partner inspected their new home. "All of those frilly curtains and such will fetch some money."

"And the garage is bigger than the one we lost," Wesley commented. "This one will hold a lot more."

Tasker grinned. "Best of all, we come out with eight dollars to the good and that's after buying beans, fatback and a pound of coffee."

"It was a shame losing that full can of Folgers, just opened it, we did."

"Dub's Place has cheese sandwiches this evening," Tasker said. "I'm hungry and this has been a rough day. Not getting blown up is reason to celebrate in my book."

"Don't let me slow you down any," Wesley said, as he accompanied his friend to their truck. "If no more exploding rats come to plague us, I'd say we're back in business."

Chapter Twenty-Eight

Tina Ortega daubed at her eyes with a white handkerchief as Barth Thornton and his newest helper wheeled the body of Henry Fossett into the morgue.

Sheriff Sinrod placed a comforting hand on Tina's shoulder. "There, there, toots, it'll be okay."

"No it won't," the nurse sobbed. "You are going to arrest me for killing Mr. Fossett. I threatened him for duping me into letting him into the morgue."

"Tina," Sam said, "if I was to go and arrest everyone who would like to have bumped that guy off, the town would have to build a bigger jail. I have a list of prime suspects as long as a telephone wire. You're not even close to being on it. Be that as it may, we still have to do our investigation and see if we can find out who killed him. The paperwork is always important."

"I didn't hit him over the head," Tina's voice firmed. "That *cabrón* I would have stabbed with a rusty knife."

The undertaker pushed the now-empty gurney through the morgue door followed by his pasty-faced young assistant who held a hand pressed to his mouth while making a dash for the bathroom.

"Good help is hard to find these days," Barth complained. "I told that idiot kid not to look at any of those jars Whitlock keeps in there." He nodded in the direction of the morgue. "The Doc's waiting for you."

Sam gave Tina a final pat on the shoulder and trudged into

the coroner's office. He was in a funk over his busted windows along with the fact that he would never be able to arrest anyone for killing Fossett. Unsolved crimes, especially murders, were things that could be used against him come next election. Provided, of course, someone chose to run against him. Given the recent spate of people burning up by themselves, the likelihood of an opponent appeared remote. Then a wonderful idea struck. His spirits buoyed, Sheriff Sinrod had a cheery smile on his face when he stepped up to the autopsy table. Dr. Whitlock was at the other side studying the corpse.

"After considering the evidence, Watson," Sam said, "I have come to the conclusion that ol' Henry here had too much to drink. Then he passed out, fell off his chair and hit his head rather fatally on a crowbar."

Dr. Whitlock looked across the table at him and cocked an eyebrow. "The first explainable death we've had in Silver City for weeks and you want to call it an *accident?*"

"It could be a good move if you give the matter some thought. For one thing, the two goons from Santa Fe might take a shine to us and add our names to their 'don't kill' list. Shucks, they'll be so thrilled and happy with us we'll probably start getting Christmas cards from them. Another point to consider is that we will never get a conviction if we pursue it, not with the state boys against us. And remember, unsolved murders always look bad on your record come election time."

Dr. Whitlock took a pack of Chesterfields from his pocket, tapped one out and lit it. After a long moment of silence he swatted a fly from Fossett's corpse and said, "The more I study the evidence, Sherlock, it becomes quite obvious to me that Henry was attempting to repair a gas leak, became overpowered by fumes, passed out and fell, fracturing his skull which caused instantaneous death."

"He doesn't have any family about that we know of. Most

people will simply be glad to have him gone. He *was* a terrible rabble-rouser and a lousy writer, to boot."

"Henry Fossett was suffering from a withered soul. The man was dying of terminal hate. Getting whacked on the head just put him out of his misery."

"I still think it would be a grand idea to go ahead and do an autopsy. It will make people think we at least spent some time studying the case."

The coroner grinned. "You can stay and help. Then we'll catch lunch at Ellie's."

Sam paled as he hurriedly stepped back from the autopsy table. "I don't have the time. I need to get over and photograph the crime . . . uh, accident . . . scene."

"See you later, Sherlock," Dr. Whitlock said to the departing sheriff.

Once the door to the morgue closed, Sam took a moment to visit with Tina. "From the way the investigation is shaping up," he said, "Fossett's death looks to be a pure accident so don't fret anymore on it."

The nurse's dark eyes widened. "Yes sir, thank you for telling me."

Tina Ortega watched the sheriff depart with feelings of amazement and relief. She was especially glad that she would be able to keep working here. Not only did she receive the excellent salary of twenty-five dollars a week, the job was anything but routine and boring. There was also the chance that the handsome Sheriff Sinrod might ask her out. All told, working in a morgue wasn't all that bad. Tina pulled a compact from her purse and began repairing the damage her earlier sobbing had wrought. There was always a chance the sheriff might return soon.

Chapter Twenty-Nine

Dr. Bryce Whitlock took a deep puff on his Chesterfield cigarette and sent a smoke ring drifting over the tops of a dozen empty beer bottles that littered their booth in Archie's Tropicana Cocktail Lounge. The coroner kept his gaze focused on the shapely derriere of departing Kathy Webster.

"Sam, my ol' buddy," Whitlock said, "there goes some real snake's hips and I think she has eyes for me."

"They're big ones, too," Sam Sinrod commented. "Betty Boop's are small compared to hers."

"Blue eyes, deep blue eyes are a wonderful attribute. They are beautiful windows to the soul."

Sheriff Sinrod knew it was definitely time to change the subject. Whenever the good doctor began waxing eloquent, not only did he know enough big words to baffle a room full of Philadelphia lawyers, he was prone to quoting Walt Whitman. To Sam's way of thinking, Whitman was the most unbelievably boring dead poet in history.

"I think," Sam said firmly, to divert his friend's train of thought, "that the boys from Santa Fe were thoroughly surprised that we ruled Henry Fossett's murder an accident."

Dr. Whitlock lowered an eyebrow. "Methinks, good sir, that you have created a new level of the oxymoron with that statement."

Sam Sinrod took a swallow of beer. Sometimes his friend's mental wheels seemed welded to their tracks. "At least no one has caught fire lately and my house didn't get blown up. That, and not being in bad graces with a couple of nasty hit men is cause for celebration in my book."

Dr. Whitlock's expression grew distant and serious. "Henry Fossett's death was a blessing, really, considering what the autopsy showed."

The sheriff straightened in his chair. "He was ill? I must say he always looked like death warmed over."

Dr. Whitlock clucked his tongue. "It was worse than that. The first thing I noticed were long healed scars on his back and buttocks from what were most likely unbelievably severe whippings he suffered as a kid. Then I discovered he had been completely castrated. Again, this was an old wound. That man had experienced a lot of pain in his life, which probably explains why he was so full of hate. But aside from all of that and being dead, Henry Fossett was healthy as a horse. It's difficult to imagine how much grief that man could have caused if he'd kept writing with that acid pen of his and inciting even more hatred. There's already too much of that to deal with. I read some of the articles he'd written but not published that I found in his desk. The world's in bad enough shape without the likes of him adding fuel to the fires of unreasoning anger."

"We can only speculate about how he got himself nutted, but I think you're saying our consciences are clear on the matter."

"Absolutely, Sam. The more I read those papers of Fossett's, the more I realized that his death was a pure accident and undeserving of our valuable time."

The sheriff brightened and took a sip of beer. "Hey, you know this is the first time in quite a while we haven't been called out because of someone burning up." He grabbed a cigar from his pocket. "I say we celebrate our little victories."

Dr. Whitlock smiled in agreement. "I can't see why not, there's only four unsolved murder cases for us to contend with now. Also, I sent a section of Officer Walker's leg off to Jim Rogers. If the chief medical examiner can't figure out what caused him to incinerate, folks shouldn't expect us to."

"And don't forget we have Lieutenant Diego and Sergeant Black to assist us."

"Yeah," Dr. Whitlock sighed. He waved an empty Carling Black Label bottle at Kathy Webster. "For that situation, Sherlock, the doctor prescribes another round."

The next morning, before the fiery sun grew too intense, Payatt Hae and his wife Chepi sat on the open porch of their adobe home shelling fresh green peas. Chepi's cousin had some land on the Gila River where water still flowed enough to support a garden, and had brought them a bushel basketful. Payatt was pondering why the gods had failed to heed his entreaties and let the white-eyes windmill dry up his spring so he could not grow any of his beloved watermelons and squash. Then Sweeney White pulled to a dusty stop with the battered old Nash automobile with which he had delivered mail for over ten years.

Payatt and Chepi stopped their task and watched stoically as the chubby mailman climbed out holding an envelope.

"Mornin', folks," Sweeney said blandly. "I've got a special delivery airmail for you from the Army. You'll need to sign for it."

Chepi stood, dumping pea hulls to the earth from her apron. She reached out and placed a thin wrinkled hand on her husband's shoulder.

The old Apache was silent a long moment then raised to stand by his wife's side. "It is about our grandson, Frank."

Payatt Hae, like many others, dreaded getting messages from the military, but he knew this was something else that must be endured. He and Chepi had raised Frank after his parents had both died from the terrible flu epidemic of years past. Frank

Hae had no other relations for the Army to deliver such a letter to.

"Don't fret about it until you read it," Sweeney said, walking over with the letter in one hand and a pen in the other. "When someone gets killed, I'm pretty sure it comes by telegram, not a letter."

Payatt Hae took the pen with a firm hand and scribbled his name where the mailman pointed. He made no attempt to take the letter.

"You'll be wanting—" Sweeney's voice trailed off when he realized the old Apache did not know how to read. "Me to read this to you."

Both Payatt and Chepi nodded solemnly.

The mailman slit the official-looking brown envelope open with his pocketknife. He studied it carefully before saying anything.

"Frank's coming home. He was hurt. His foot's broken, he's bruised and has a rupture, but he'll recover just fine given a little time. He is being honorably discharged from the Army because of his injuries. The Colonel Bridgeport who wrote this said a five-hundred-pound bomb got loose and Frank stopped its rolling with his body. He goes on to say your grandson saved a lot of soldiers' lives with his quick thinking. They're also giving him a long list of medals including the Purple Heart."

Payatt's stoic expression remained. "This bad thing happened to Frank because he was in a land where it does not snow. Nothing good could happen in such a place. I am glad he is leaving there and coming home. It will snow here this winter."

Sweeney White understood that the venerable Apache did not look at things the same way normal folks did. But he was glad for the old folks' sake that the news wasn't devastating. The carrier folded the letter, replaced it in the official-looking envelope and handed it to Payatt Hae.

"It'll be nice to have Frank back on the sheriff's department," he said. "I'm sure Sam Sinrod'll be happy to hear the news."

Payatt reached out, took the envelope, then glared up the gentle canyon. "When my grandson gets home, it will be good. The gods who saved his life may now have time to help me flatten a windmill."

When Sweeney climbed back into his battered car, he noticed the venerable old couple were back to shelling peas once again, in complete silence. He thought on the matter and decided there really was nothing more that needed saying. There was a lot to be said for the Apache culture. His wife, Bertha, never seemed to shut up.

Sweeney White pushed in the clutch, ground the Nash into gear and headed off, leaving a cloud of oil smoke and gray powder dust hanging in the still, hot air.

Chapter Thirty

"You know, it's been a long while since we've seen a promising bank of rain clouds in the west," Sam Sinrod commented as he and Bryce Whitlock walked across the torrid concrete parking lot to the dining room of the Copper Mountain Hotel. "Way too long."

"Strange things like that can happen on odd days like this one's shaping up to be," the coroner tapped a Chesterfield from a gold case and lit it. "Garret Black and Neto Diego inviting us to lunch has to go down as an exceptionally odd occurrence, especially in a public place where any poison they might slip into our food would attract attention."

The sheriff stopped mid-step. "You're kidding, right?"

Whitlock chuckled. "I'm betting those two will be friendly as pet bears now that we let them get away with murder. The worst those nice hit men are going to do is add our bill to their state expense account. I doubt if anyone doing accounting in Santa Fe dares to question their expenses too closely. Today we get a free lunch. Tomorrow, however, might be a totally different story."

Sam Sinrod said, "Some years back there used to be a man living up Stonehouse Canyon who had a pet cinnamon bear. He'd gotten it when it was just a cub and raised it with a bottle. That bear was so tame little kids could ride around on it like it was a pony. Then one day a neighbor found the guy ripped to pieces. It turned out that bear had gutted him for some reason.

A bear has claws that can be four or five inches long, nice sharp ones, too. You know they never did find that bear, or so I was told."

"I've been in Silver City long enough to expect that sooner or later it'll turn up." Dr. Whitlock took a second to stare at the approaching storm clouds after hearing a peal of distant thunder. "Let's go eat, I'm famished."

Sergeant Black and Lieutenant Diego sat side by side at the center of two tables that were placed end-to-end and covered with one long white tablecloth.

The coroner was briefly reminded of Leonardo da Vinci's painting of the Last Supper, but decided it would be best to keep the comparison to himself. Undoubtedly, however, the vision of those two were the last thing a lot of people ever saw on this earth.

"Welcome, my friends," Neto said without standing. "Take a chair and order anything on the menu. We are most happy that you could join us."

"Thanks for asking us," Sam said cheerfully. "I trust you gentlemen are enjoying your visit to our fair city."

"I must say that no one's caught fire since *we've* been here," Black said in his normal deep voice that sounded like a growl coming from the dark depths of a cave.

"And I want you to know we're very appreciative," the coroner said, taking a chair across the table from the sergeant. He picked up a menu and asked, "How do you like the steaks here?"

The sergeant glared daggers at Dr. Whitlock while Neto, who appeared oblivious to the doctor's jibe, began a long discourse on which variety of steaks were the most tender.

"You know I had most of my stomach blown away by a shotgun blast," Garret Black said harshly. "I can only eat raw eggs these days."

"A woman shot him in Texas," Neto added. "It's easy for anyone to get shot in that state. She mistook him for another man who did harm to her husband. The matter was a most unfortunate circumstance."

"I'm sorry to hear about that," Dr. Whitlock said in a sympathetic tone. "I would imagine, Sergeant, that such a healthy diet as yours becomes quite boring over time."

"Nah," Garret said with a shrug. "I got used to it."

An hour later, after Lieutenant Diego added an entire apple pie along with a pint of vanilla ice cream to the two huge T-bone steaks along with baked potatoes and all the trimmings he had wolfed down, the men sat back and observed one another over coffee.

"The governor has asked us to stay and investigate the cases of spontaneous human combustion that happened here," Neto said in a strangely cordial tone. "Apparently a Mrs. Guttman, whose husband was a contributor to his political party, phoned him. She is a *most* generous contributor, I should add."

Sam nodded. "Percy was her husband's name. He was a pharmacist and a nice little guy who was simply out rabbit hunting. We found his boots with feet still in them where a brushfire began."

"He went and burnt up just like that junk dealer did in *Bleak House,*" Sergeant Black said.

"Yeah," Sam said with a nod. "All of our four cases went up in flames exactly like that Krook fellow did. Spontaneous human combustion has been around for a while."

Neto said while picking his teeth, "I think we would do well to keep focused on the here and now." He eyed the coroner. "Does anyone have a clue what causes this? Sergeant Black and I are of the opinion that it must be something in the water. Officer Walker was sampling water at the time of his demise, I believe."

Sam Sinrod coughed to clear his throat. "Uh, yeah—sampling was what he was doing when he caught fire."

"No one's burnt up since," Black added firmly. "Maybe it's all over; the water might have got better on its own for some reason."

"Officer Walker was the last to die," the sheriff said. "I'm hoping, as are you, that there will be no more cases for us to worry over."

"We will stay here in Silver City for a while, and wait to see what happens—" Neto's voice trailed off as the sound of wailing sirens in the distance took his along with everyone else's attention.

"That sounds like Freeman's fire truck and the pumper, for sure," Sam said, sliding his chair back and jumping up. "The other siren's Burke Martin's cruiser. Something bad has gone and happened."

"At least we were able to enjoy a nice quiet lunch before being so rudely interrupted," Neto Diego said. He stood with a grunt. "The sergeant and I will come along to see what the matter is."

"Maybe something simply got struck by lightning," Sam ventured as they headed for the door. "There was a big storm coming our way from out of the west when we got here."

"Let's just hope that's what it is," Dr. Whitlock added.

When the four lawmen exited the restaurant, they stood in bright hot sunshine. A scattering of black clouds over the rounded hills to the south showed that the hoped-for rainstorm had changed direction and was now heading for Mexico.

Then Barth Thornton's hearse came roaring by following the town marshal, Hap Johnson, who was driving his battered Dodge cruiser with a flashing red light on its roof. The old car's siren had not worked for years.

"If it's bad enough to get Hap out, suffering from gout the way he is, I'd expect something terrible has happened," Sheriff Sinrod commented.

The group turned to study the direction where the hearse and patrol car were heading. In the distance, flashing red lights began circling the ornate two-story brick-and-marble building that housed the St. Mary's Catholic Church.

Sam and the coroner exchanged somber glances.

Garret Black wore the first semblance of a smile they had seen. The skinny, silver-haired sergeant's eyes sparked gray-green, like old ice. "Let's go see who got toasted," he said gleefully.

Chapter Thirty-One

The stench of burnt flesh was nearly overpowering in the confines of the small room on the second floor of the convent. Only a few of the men who had rushed to the scene lingered any longer than was absolutely necessary. This case of spontaneous human combustion was worse than any of the others. Far worse.

"There's quite a lot of her left," Sam Sinrod rasped, breathing through his mouth in an attempt to suppress the rising bile.

"I don't know for how much longer," Dr. Whitlock said in the detached tone of a scientist describing some experiment gone awry. "Whatever is causing the immolation is still active, it's working away at incinerating what's left."

The sheriff backed up as close to the door as he could. He sincerely regretted eating a huge fried ham steak for lunch. Sam was also wishing for a jar of camphor to smear under his nose to help quench his building nausea.

Everyone present kept their focus on the smoking corpse of a very old woman that lay on a small bed alongside the far wall. The body was in two pieces, the upper chest with its ghastly contorted face and arms that splayed outward, palms up as if from a supplicant. Then there were the lower hips and legs. Where the middle part of the body should have been was a blackened, smouldering mass.

Sparks, along with occasional fingers of orange flame snapped and played along the edges of the open chest cavity.

Garret Black stepped close to the corpse, obviously fixated by what was transpiring. "Look at that. It's like electricity and it's still eating away at what's left." He clucked his tongue and grinned malevolently. "This is remarkable, truly remarkable."

"You'd best keep your distance, Sergeant," the coroner snapped. "We don't have any idea what it is we are dealing with here. For all we know it might be catching."

Sergeant Black kept his full attention on the smoking corpse, a malignant grin frozen on his lips. "I *really* want to know how this was done." The state trooper stepped even closer, reached out and placed an index finger to where fiery sparks were playing along the sternum bone. Small jagged bolts of electricity jumped to his finger. To everyone's amazement, Black did not jerk away. The evil smile on his sunken, pale face grew in intensity. It was as if he was actually feeding off the lightning-like flames that began crackling and sparking up his hand. Dr. Whitlock drew his right arm back and slapped Garret's hand away from the corpse.

"What in hell did you do that for?" Black growled. "That ain't nothing but a little electricity, hardly even shocked me. The sensation was more of a tickle than anything."

"You had better hope it is only common electricity. I've never even heard of that eating away at flesh like this is doing." Dr. Whitlock glared at the skinny sergeant and added, "Have you?"

Black held his finger in front of his face and studied it intently. "Not regular electric I haven't. This stuff seems different than the regular electric that runs through power lines. Causes more of a tickle than anything. But what I want to know is how it's been altered and—" his voice trailed off.

Loud popping noises from the corpse caused Garret Black along with everyone else in the room to jump back. The fingers of flames began growing in length and intensity, now from both sections of the body, sizzling and hissing like bacon in a hot skillet. In the span of brief seconds the entire corpse was consumed in front of startled eyes.

Dr. Whitlock observed, "This time even the feet were burned up. There's only ashes left of that woman. And it happened right in front of us."

"Amazing," Garret Black said, obviously elated. "To only know how this was done and be able to cause it to happen would be wonderful. Simply wonderful."

Lieutenant Diego noticed the sheriff and undertaker staring at his friend. "The sergeant means it would be wonderful to know how to solve this case. He has difficulties, on occasion, expressing himself correctly."

Smoke from the conflagration began drifting toward the men.

"I think we should take off and let the room air out. There's nothing anyone can do here anyway," Sam Sinrod said. "The bed and floor's already been wet down, nothing else is going to burn that hasn't already."

"I agree," Barth Thornton and the coroner said in unison, already spinning to leave the stench.

Less than a moment later, only Garret Black remained in the room. The sergeant had gone back to alongside the bed, studying the ashes with the intensity of a surgeon examining a wound. Neither the thin tendrils of gray smoke drifting about his head nor the terrible foul odor appeared to bother him in the least.

"The sergeant may want to stay and study the scene for some time. He is quite dedicated to his work," Neto Diego said as he accompanied the sheriff down the stairs.

"I've noticed that," Sam replied hoarsely, still fighting building nausea. "I surely have."

Father Pedro Mondragon knelt facing the altar. He chanted a prayer in Latin while nervously thumbing a string of rosary beads. The venerable old priest had been in Silver City as far back as anyone could remember. He was a kindly man who spoke fluently in both Spanish and English. His many deeds of charity and compassion had garnered him the respect and admiration of both cultures.

Sheriff Sinrod stepped alongside the priest while he awaited the end of his prayers. Sam thought the myriad lines on Father Mondragon's leathery face had deepened. It was as if death left a scar on the old patriarch's face every time he visited. And lately, it seemed, the Grim Reaper had favored this mountain hamlet they called home.

"*Señor* Sheriff," the priest said, struggling to stand on bony legs that creaked from the effort. "I do not know what happened to Sister Ignacia. I have never seen or even heard of such a terrible thing before."

"I'd venture very few people have, Father," Sam said. "We call it spontaneous human combustion. This is the fifth case to occur here in Silver City."

"Yes, *Señor* Sheriff, I know. Those unfortunates from the traveling medicine show who are staying with us lost their banjo player to the same malady that took our sister."

Dr. Whitlock stepped up holding a well-worn leather notebook. "Padre, I'm going to need her full name and particulars . . . for the record."

The priest nodded sadly. "I understand, my son, Sister Ignacia Lopez would have been one hundred and one years old this November. She has been at St. Mary's even longer than I, coming here in eighteen seventy-two. That was seventy-one years ago. I have been ministering to the souls of Silver City since only eighteen ninety-nine, a mere forty-four years."

The coroner swallowed, he was never comfortable with these types of questions. "That was a very long time indeed, Padre. I'm going to need to know if she has relatives. And is there anyone we should notify of her passing?"

A sigh passed the priest's lips. "No, my son, Sister Ignacia had only her church and her God. I believe that her demise has already been noted by the one who matters."

"This is only for the records."

"Of course, Dr. Whitlock, I understand matters of law. The good sister had become quite infirm and has not been outside the convent for many years. The rhubarb wine she so enjoyed, she made from stalks the parishioners brought to her."

Sam Sinrod blinked. "I've never even heard of rhubarb wine."

"It is an acquired taste, *Señor* Sheriff, you are quite welcome to take what bottles remain, as I am certain no one else will want them."

Whitlock lowered his notebook. "Padre, what we just witnessed up there goes beyond any science that I'm familiar with. I honestly don't know what to make of people burning up without reason. But I really doubt rhubarb wine was the cause."

"God's purpose is often hidden from the eyes of mortals, but it will be ultimately revealed to the patient. You may have Mr. Thornton remove the ashes. Sister Ignacia's soul has fled them. I shall say Mass for the dead, you men must investigate the cause. Each one of us have our tasks in sad times such as these."

"Father," Sam said, "I sure hope you're right about us eventually finding out what caused this to happen."

"Trust in the Lord, my son, he will cause the scales to fall from the eyes of the believer."

The sheriff and coroner turned to watch as Sergeant Black came clumping down the stairs. He still wore a sinister smile on his narrow face.

"In God, I'll trust," Sam Sinrod said to the old padre. "But He's at the head of a mighty short list." Then he turned and went outside to talk with the undertaker.

Chapter Thirty-Two

The chalk gave a nerve-racking screech when Sheriff Sam Sinrod finished writing the last name on the blackboard. He winced as he turned to face the assemblage he had called together in his office to discuss the strange course of the immolations that were plaguing the town of Silver City.

"Gentlemen," Sam said, sweeping his arm across the small blackboard that sat on a wobbly tripod. "This is a list I have put together of known victims of human combustion, beginning with the first." He stepped aside to study his handiwork along with everyone else.

(1) Phil Pegler—Prophet—drinker—lived in a cave
(2) Percy Guttman—Rabbit hunter—teetotaler
(3) Parmenter Jones—Banjo player—heavy drinker—new to town—colored
(4) Roan Walker—Arson investigator—from out of town—white
(5) Sister Ignacia Lopez—100 y/o Nun—drank rhubarb wine—Mexican

The sheriff continued, "What we have to look for here is some common thread to connect all of these people with whatever the hell caused them to catch on fire."

"Three of the names begin with the letter 'P'," District Attorney Norbert Pike ventured.

"Something *useful* would be a tad more what we have in mind," Dr. Whitlock said standing alongside the sheriff.

"Seems like whatever the hell it is," Fire Chief Bates commented, "it's equal opportunity."

"Yeah," Deputy Martin said. "Percy not being a drinker or smoker sure put holes in a lot of great theories."

Norbert Pike snorted. "If drinking and smoking caused people to burn up from spontaneous human combustion, there wouldn't be enough folks left in Grant County to hold a game of poker."

"Two of the victims were from out of town," Sam Sinrod said, in an attempt to keep the meeting focused. "The banjo player had only been here a couple of days. Officer Walker, just a few hours."

The district attorney consulted his notes. "I see Mr. Jones was on a stage playing his banjo when he lit off. Now our arson investigator appeared to be—"

"Sampling water," Dr. Whitlock interrupted, while turning to face Lieutenant Neto Diego and Sergeant Black who were standing next to the door.

"Don't bother," Neto Diego said with a dismissive wave of his right hand. "We know Officer Walker was doing push-ups over some broad in Madame Millie's when he burnt up. That guy was like a dog that broke its leash whenever he got out of town. Everyone we talked to except the local law told us what really happened. It came as no surprise to us. Roan Walker was a man who suffered bad from squirrel fever. I'd reckon that ain't nothing to be ashamed of, actually."

Hap Johnson, the aged town marshal, cocked his silver-cropped head thoughtfully. "Yep, I remember those days. But I sure don't recollect anything about 'em that burnt more than a hole in my wallet. The folks on that blackboard took burning up serious."

"Parmenter Jones, the banjo player, caught on fire in front of over fifty people," Sam Sinrod said in a desperate attempt to keep everyone's mental train on its tracks. "The Prophet was in Dub's Place drinking a beer when he went up in smoke, lots of folks saw that happen, too. What we have to do is connect the dots and find out what caused these cases to happen."

Sergeant Black stared at his index finger. "It's electricity that's doing it. I think if enough of the stuff built up in a body, like in a battery, the result would be an overload and cause 'em to burn right up like that nun did this afternoon."

Dr. Whitlock said, "Percy Guttman was out in a field hunting rabbits. How did he get an electric charge into his system? There were no power lines anywhere close to where he lit off."

"Ol' Percy sure went and caused one helluva brushfire," Freeman Bates added. "Damn near burnt down the whole town, would have too, if the wind had been from out of the south."

"I *felt* it," Garret Black growled. "I know what electricity is. This stuff is different for some reason. What I don't know is how to make it build up enough to burn someone up, but I'm going to find out. Most likely the cause will be found in the science of electrochemistry applied to thermodynamics."

Dr. Whitlock and the sheriff stared blankly at each other. They both had suspected the largest words in the sergeant's vocabulary would be of the more pragmatic variety like "disembowel" or possibly "strychnine."

Lieutenant Diego flicked the back of his hand to his companion. "He reads a lot of books."

Sam Sinrod stifled a sigh. He had five cases of spontaneous human combustion to solve. Hell, he didn't even know if they were murders, suicides or some strange new disease. Now a hit man from Santa Fe was trying to muddle things up even more by using words big enough to stump Einstein while spouting off things about electricity no one understood. What Sam needed was something concrete to put on paper to make these problems go away. Then he could return to solving crimes that could be found in law books.

"I once had me an uncle on my pappy's side," Hap Johnson said, hoisting his right foot across his leg. He had sliced his shoe open to allow his big toe, which from gout was the size of an apple, to have some room. "Tried to build a perpetual motion machine. He was always using big words like that. Wilbur was his name and he was an idiot, plain and simple. Ol' Wilbur never knew what any of these big words meant, just used 'em to impress folks. The contraption he built never did do more than scare the cat."

"Common threads," Sheriff Sinrod said trying not to sound desperate. "That's what we need to find, some element to connect all of the victims. Then we might be able to trace down the cause, whatever the hell it is."

"They all burnt up from an overload of electricity," Garret Black affirmed. "We just don't know how it was done . . . yet."

Dr. Whitlock said, "I think the sergeant here may be correct. The biggest piece we've recovered from anyone was most of Officer Walker's left leg. I observed black or burnt jagged lines radiating outward from the femur bone that could have been caused by electric current. I sliced off a section of Walker's leg and sent it to the state medical examiner's office in Santa Fe. We have not heard back from them as to what they found."

"Okay, okay!" Sam boomed. "If it turns out to be electricity, that is fine. What we *need* to do is connect the dots to see how they got exposed to it in the first place so we can stop others from burning up."

"Sheriff Sinrod's correct, gentlemen," Norbert Pike said. "We can't expect to allow this sort of thing to continue and us get elected again. Whatever it is, we've got to bring this mess to a halt or plan on being out of a job."

"I ain't gonna run again," Hap Johnson said, massaging his infected toe. "Gettin' too old."

"There is one common denominator that I can see." Lieutenant Diego's words brought a silence to the room where a person could hear a pin drop.

"Yes," the sheriff said hopefully. "Go ahead."

"Remains from each of the deceased were taken to Mr. Thornton's funeral parlor."

Barth snorted, then grinned evilly. "I'm the only mortician in Grant County. And I maintain an open-door policy . . . every *body* is welcome."

A chorus of low groans drifted across the assemblage. People shuffled their feet, staring out the windows at a glowing red cloudless sunset.

"I was just trying to be helpful," Neto Diego mumbled.

"It's getting late," the district attorney announced, scooting back his chair and standing. "Since we've been conducting business, the county will pick up everyone's dinner at the Copper Mountain."

"Hey, this is fried-chicken night, too," Freeman Bates added cheerfully. "And it comes with mashed potatoes and cream gravy along with pie for dessert."

"Can't eat chicken, bothers my gout," Hap Johnson said, struggling to stand. "But I'll hobble over an' check out the menu. Maybe they'll have trout. Now that don't bother my infected toe at all for some reason."

Dr. Whitlock and Sheriff Sinrod stood by the blackboard and watched as the room emptied in less than a minute.

"Well, *that* was a fruitful meeting," the coroner said sarcastically. "We are really beginning to make progress solving those cases."

"There's one thing for certain."

"What's that, Sherlock?"

"Norbert Pike will never make the mistake of asking Lieutenant Diego out to dinner again. That man could bankrupt Rockefeller with his appetite, let alone the budget Grant County has to work with."

"Then let's go join 'em while the county's still got enough money to pay for it."

Chapter Thirty-Three

Sheriff Sinrod and the coroner had just reached the bottom of the worn sandstone steps leading to his office when a 1933 Ford Model C wood-body station wagon pulling a green and yellow enclosed trailer chugged to a stop in front of the men.

Bubbles the clown from the burned-out medicine show was driving, but it took them a moment to recognize him without his red nose and wearing a brown bowler hat. Then the two doors on the far side swung open, Pres Darby along with Suzy Clay climbed out and walked around the car to visit.

Sam gave a hard swallow when he noticed the shapely Indian girl still wore a skimpy tan leather halter top that bared her trim middle. Suzy's ample charms jiggled enticingly as she flowed like quicksilver to stand in front of him.

"We wanted to stop by and thank you for your kindness, Sheriff," Pres Darby said, offering a hand. "I know you asked us to stick around for a while, but after what happened to that poor nun today, we're leaving this town."

Sam Sinrod had not noticed Darby's presence. He quickly took the proffered hand. "That's . . . that's understandable—" he stammered.

"You folks have had a rough time here," Bryce Whitlock said stepping close. The coroner knew that the presence of the sensuous dancer had effectively reduced his friend's vocabulary to single, halting words or an embarrassing mewing sound. Sexy girls always did that to the sheriff. He would have to be the one to carry on any coherent conversation.

"Ain't that the truth," Bubbles said from inside the car. "Our medicine show, all of our money, and our banjo player all got burned up."

Doc Darby motioned to the colorful trailer. "We managed to scrounge over a hundred dollars in silver coins from where the truck burnt. Then Bubbles offered to help with a little money he had managed to stash away. I reckon we've got ourselves a new start if we can just get out of Silver City before some other disaster strikes."

"Come and look," Suzy Clay squealed happily, heading for the trailer. "See our new attraction."

Sam Sinrod nearly tripped on his way to see what they had to show them, but the coroner grabbed him in time to save humiliation.

The gaudy trailer was painted with huge red letters:

SEE THE MAN EATING CHICKEN 10 cents
ASK ABOUT THE ROSICRUCIAN FAITH (AMORC) BOOKS
10 cents

Dr. Whitlock's astonishment was obviously genuine. "A man-eating chicken?"

"Yeah," Pres Darby shrugged. "It'll only cost 'em a thin dime to peek in the trailer to see Bubbles gnawing away on a drumstick. Most folks will get a chuckle out of it. I'll go back to selling my Elixir of Life once I can afford to buy the ingredients."

Sam Sinrod surprised his friend by managing to ask, "What's Rosy-crucians?"

"It's an old, mystic and secret religious order," Suzy Clay answered smiling seductively, which brought a red glow to the sheriff's face. "All of the secrets of life and happiness may be found in a single book that costs a mere dime."

"We got ourselves a real good deal on seven boxes of 'em,"

Pres Darby added. "A couple of old guys who drive a Model A pickup truck sold them to us really cheap. You folks can have a copy if you want one. After today I'd venture being a Rosicrucian's safer than being a Catholic."

"That's okay," Whitlock said cocking his head. "You'd best sell them. The sheriff and I will muddle along like we have been. Too much religion isn't good for a person."

"Umerer," Sam mumbled, staring at Suzy's halter top. "Er . . . er . . . er."

"The sheriff means to say we're late for a dinner appointment," the coroner said cheerfully. "By the way, where are you folks headed?"

"California sounds like it will be a good place to recoup." Pres Darby wrapped an arm around Suzy's slender waist. "There's a wonderful mix of money and idiots over there, great for our type of business, so that's where we're heading. I've also never heard of folks burning up in California, either, which will be a solid improvement over New Mexico."

Dr. Whitlock frowned in exasperation. "We honestly don't have a clue why those people caught on fire like they did."

"And I ain't planning to stick around to see if it's spreading," Bubbles hollered. "That nun going up in holy smoke was the last straw. I'm for getting the hell outta Silver City and not letting any grass grow under my feet doing it."

Pres Darby's voice carried a hint of annoyance. "Bubbles has an odd tendency to mess up words. That's why I do all of the hawking, but we had best be off. After all, the trailer and car are his and, as you can see, Bubbles is in a real dither to get out of New Mexico."

"Well, lots of luck to you folks and have a safe trip," Dr. Whitlock said, stepping aside to allow the pair to pass.

Sheriff Sinrod managed a wave as the old station wagon towing a gaudy trailer began chugging up the slight hill to the highway, leaving a cloud of blue oil smoke in its wake.

"Now you can resume speaking English, Sherlock," Whitlock said with a grin. "The pretty girl has gone bye-bye."

"I was just taken aback is all. Women running around half-naked isn't a normal occurrence around here."

"That's why you can get along without an interpreter. Let's get over to the Copper Mountain before Lieutenant Diego cleans the kitchen out."

Sam took a longing last look at the car that was departing into the red flare of a dying sun. Then he spun and hurried to join his friend who was already a block away.

Chapter Thirty-Four

The morning was shaping up to be a carbon copy of too many scorching, cloudless days that had parched southwest New Mexico. Not a hint of the life-giving rain clouds that had tantalized the drought-stricken area yesterday could be seen, having fled like the promise of a strumpet.

It was just past seven a.m. and already the temperature inside Ellie's Diner showed well over ninety degrees on a wall thermometer. A pair of slow-moving ceiling fans seemed to only swirl the hot stale air, cigarette smoke and myriad greenflies about. The pungent smell of old grease sizzling on a huge, flat cast-iron grill hung heavy as fog in the oppressive heat.

"What's good to eat for breakfast here?" Neto Diego asked gleefully studying the menu on the wall. "I am totally famished."

Dr. Whitlock forced back a look of utter amazement. In medical school he had learned that the human stomach is elastic, expanding to hold food, but none of the professors nor medical books had ever truly indicated the immense limits to which it could be stretched by a dedicated glutton, such as Lieutenant Neto Diego.

Sergeant Black glowered at the table. "I'm going to have six raw eggs in a glass with some garlic juice and hot chili sauce. The way things are going I should add a shot of whiskey, but I ain't. There's thinking that needs done and I'm serious about finding out how people can burn up by electricity. I need my wits about me."

Sam Sinrod simply wanted to get this meeting over with. The smell of fried foods he found repugnant, doubting if he could digest even a stack of sourdough pancakes. What the two hit men wanted to meet about could surely have waited. Lieutenant Diego had phoned him at six, shaking him from a most pleasant dream involving a beautiful, raven-haired Indian girl, to invite him to breakfast. He now regretted mentioning meeting here at Ellie's. The Copper Mountain had one of those new evaporative air coolers that would surely have dispersed the awful smell of frying meat. The only good thing to come of the call was that he had given Lieutenant Diego the coroner's phone number which had successfully wrecked Dr. Whitlock's sleep, too.

"You gentlemen wanted to discuss something?" Sam asked, sipping a steaming cup of coffee.

"Ah yes, Sheriff," Neto Diego said keeping his eyes focused on the menu. "The sergeant is in a foul mood because we must be on our way to Hobbs to take care of an . . . ah . . . rather pressing matter there."

"That's mighty blasted close to the damn state of Texas," Garret Black grumbled. "I really hate that place. I got shot in Texas, you know."

"I believe you mentioned that, Sergeant," Dr. Whitlock said. His voice grew silvery, "Do be careful."

"I intend to do just that." Sergeant Black clucked his tongue as he reached across the table and stuck a beet red index finger at the coroner. "Take a gander at this, Doc. The thing's gotten all blistery and flaky. It kind of itches a lot, too."

Dr. Whitlock quickly slid his cup of coffee from under Garret's finger. The coroner cocked his head as he studiously scrutinized the obviously red and blistered digit.

"The doctor told you not to touch that nun," Lieutenant Diego scolded. "You should have listened to him."

"I just wanted to make sure it was electricity," Black snorted. "A person has to know what it is to make it happen."

Sam Sinrod nipped a sigh by running the edge of his hand across his pencil-thin moustache. Only now did it dawn on him that Sergeant Black's fascination with spontaneous human combustion was to be able to cause it to happen to others. He should have realized this earlier. In Garret's line of endeavor, it would be a valuable tool to cause people to incinerate while he was hundreds of miles away amongst numerous witnesses when the event occurred.

"It appears to mimic a bad sunburn," Dr. Whitlock said in a professional tone. "Perhaps rubbing on some lotion might help with the itching, but I think your finger will heal in a few days. The edges of the blisters are already showing new skin growth."

"See," Garret said to Neto as he retrieved his hand. "I told you it was only electric current, plain and simple."

"I'm so happy for you," Lieutenant Diego said smiling broadly at Ellie who stood at the table holding an order pad. "We should have our breakfast and be on our way. Duty calls."

"What'll it be, boys?" Ellie asked, causing the ash from her cigarette to fall onto the floor.

Neto cocked his head in deep thought. "Two orders of bacon and hash browns with three eggs each, over easy. A stack of sourdough pancakes with a side of ham. Then a Spanish omelet with lots of jalapeno peppers, two of those delicious-looking sweet rolls and a couple of large glasses of milk." He hesitated. "Oh yeah, add some wheat toast; two orders with plenty of strawberry jelly."

Ellie took a moment to jot everything down. "It'll be right out." She turned to leave.

"Excuse me," Sam Sinrod called after her. "But the rest of us would like to order some breakfast, too."

★ ★ ★ ★ ★

Looking through the front windows of Ellie's Diner, Sam Sinrod and the coroner watched as a huge black 1936 Packard carrying the pair of hit men known as "the Janitors" roared off, leaving a cloud of gray dust hanging in the torrid air.

Dr. Whitlock turned his attention to a steaming cup of coffee. "It's been said that some people bring pleasure by coming, and others by going. Seeing those two creeps heading out of town gives me a downright good feeling."

Sam kept staring out the window, his face a mask of frozen stillness. "They're going to kill someone," he said simply.

Whitlock sipped at his coffee. "Cheer up. It won't happen in Grant County and there's always the distinct possibility they'll whack a person who desperately needs it. Hit men generally don't go after the pure in heart, if you think on the matter."

"Yeah, I suppose I should just be glad they've gone and concentrate on trying to figure out why all those voters went up in flames like they did."

"That's what Garret Black wants to know, too. For him it'd be a boon, he'd give his right arm to be able to cause folks to catch fire."

The sheriff's dark eyes sparked. "*Someone's* right arm, anyway."

"No," Dr. Whitlock said, his voice serious. "I mean his own arm. Those strange blisters on his finger are like nothing I've ever seen. Hell, I've never even seen pictures in medical books that showed clusters of white speckled blisters like he has. I honestly don't know if the damage will spread or not."

Sam nearly choked on a swallow of coffee. "You told him it was nothing!"

The doctor's expression was one of smug satisfaction. "Yes," the coroner said cheerfully, "I know I did."

Chapter Thirty-Five

Payatt Hae could not help but wonder if possibly some of the small gods had been around the white-eyes for too long and had lost their minds. This would explain much.

The venerable old Apache sat in a spindly cane rocker under a veranda over the back door to his adobe home. It felt good to be out of the sun, which was growing hotter by the moment. Payatt smiled when he remembered back on the time that he and his grandson, Frank, had built the shelter using thorny mesquite and ocotillo branches. It would be good to have Frank home again, out of South Pacific where it did not snow and men were shooting at him. At least the gods had been kind and saw to it that he had not been killed in that faraway land where a spirit could become lost.

Payatt sipped at a cup of hot chocolate, which he considered to be the most excellent thing the white-eyes had brought to The People. But, like everything else in these hard times, it had to be paid for with money, something he was growing quite short of.

If the *Pinda-lik-o-yi* windmill had not dried up his spring, the cattle would be fat and he could sell them for some of this needed money. Instead they were skinny. They also were eating hay he had to buy while they drank water that he bought from the city and was forced to carry in a big tank on the back of his pickup truck. The truck also ate a lot of expensive gasoline which he could only buy a few gallons of because of what they called "rationing." No, things were not good for The People.

All in all, it would be better for the Apache to return to the old ways. Payatt knew however, this would never be. The old ways were gone forever. Even the young Sheriff Sinrod, who his grandson called a friend, had told him to shoot a deer only when the white-eyes' law said they were "in season," or do it at night when he could not see it happen. The white-eyes' laws were too plentiful to understand. The Apache were accustomed to shooting deer when they were hungry, not when some law said it was all right.

Yes, Payatt Hae mused, the times were strange and strange things were happening on the distant hill where the hated windmill sat that had sucked the life-giving water from his spring and caused him to spend money for what the gods had always provided for free.

The great god *Usen* should have smashed that windmill with his first fireball. Payatt had now danced three *Gahe*s, yet the windmill still stood and his spring was still dry. No, he was surely dealing with small gods, not the Great *Usen.*

And the small gods, whose minds had been muddled by the white-eyes, were obviously confused as to how to destroy a windmill. They had buzzed about, looking it over with red eyes. In the darkest part of last night he had heard the beating of great wings, but when he ran to look, he could see nothing. It had been a spirit eagle, most likely.

Payatt finished the delicious hot chocolate and finally managed to stand on legs that hurt and did not work as they had when he was young. This, however, was as things were supposed to be. Payatt was old, soon it would be time for him to go to the Spirit World. Once there, he would make a point of asking the great *Usen* why he had caused him grief and not flattened that windmill. Payatt Hae had done nothing to offend a god.

The day was growing hot. Payatt needed to empty the water

tank for the cattle, then slide the heavy metal container off the pickup truck to make room in the bed for them to go shopping. Chepi wanted him to drive her into Silver City and take her to many stores. This was something he dreaded. It was always more work than building fences from rocks or chopping wood.

Payatt sighed. The trip would also use up much money. Chepi had developed a fondness for the white-eyes' stores and had a tendency to go crazy there. His wife of many summers would examine a thing in one store, then go to another and examine exactly the same thing. Then, Chepi would most certainly go back to the first store and buy exactly what she had first seen. It was sad when a person lost their mind.

The old Apache decided that if his wife bought more cocoa the effort could be worthwhile. Then, he sighed and thought once again of that hated windmill. He would dance yet another *Gahe* to *Usen.* This time however, he would yell out to *Usen* many times. The great god may have much to keep his attention elsewhere. With a war going on, persistence might be needed for *Usen* himself to answer. Some loud yelling might get the attention he needed.

Payatt Hae set aside the old and chipped cup that was now empty, then hobbled slowly to go drain the precious water he had bought with his dwindling supply of money. He intended to be quite careful not to spill a single drop. The more he tarried, the less time Chepi would have to go crazy and spend money in stores. This was an added incentive to be thrifty.

CHAPTER THIRTY-SIX

When Sam Sinrod came into his office he found Burke Martin leaning back in his chair, feet propped up on the sheriff's desk, snoring loudly. A copy of *Official Detective* magazine was splayed open across Burke's ample belly.

Sam gave an emphatic cough which did not so much as change the pitch of his deputy's wheezing snorts. He doubted if a gunshot would wake the man. Burke Martin was noted for slipping into what Dr. Whitlock would describe as a coma whenever he dozed off.

To save time and recover his chair, Sam walked around the desk and shook the deputy's shoulder. Burke snorted like a startled hog. His eyes fluttered open. The chubby deputy grunted, slid his feet off the sheriff's desk and bolted upright, the magazine spilling to the floor.

"Uh . . . mornin', Sheriff," Burke sputtered groggily. "I was studying police procedures and must have dozed off. I was up late last night thinkin' about ways to make the department more efficient."

"A tad more efficiency around here would be a good place to start." Sam eyed the top of his desk for notes. Happily, none were visible. "I take it nothing new has happened."

"Nope, those five unsolved cases of people burning up is all I know of."

The sheriff suppressed a groan and plopped down into his oak swivel chair. If he was not successful in figuring out how to at least stop this spate of immolations, he wouldn't have to ponder any longer over whether or not moving to Montana and becoming a shoe salesman might be a good career move. The decision would be made for him by the voters of Grant County, New Mexico.

Sam unlocked a desk drawer, took out a long black Cuban cigar from a drawer and lit it. "The folks from Doc Darby's medicine show left town after that nun burnt up yesterday."

"They were staying at St. Mary's Church, weren't they?"

"Yes, I'm the one who sent them there. Those people were living in the truck that burned and they had no other place to go and they were broke."

Burke Martin yawned. "We might should have made them stay in town until all those deaths are solved. Those people were hereabouts when two of 'em burnt up, you know."

Sam took a long puff on his cigar. "I agree, it'd been better if they stuck around, but there's no charges we could hold them on. I don't think they'll be hard to find if we have to go looking for them. Burke, we don't even begin to know why those people caught fire and burnt up like they did. It might be some kind of natural phenomenon we're unaware of. We can't jump to the conclusion that a crime has been committed until we have some evidence to back us up."

The deputy cocked his head in thought. "Yeah, I reckon, but that Princess Nubia was sure one hot patootie, wasn't she?"

Sam's head dropped slightly. "Yes, Burke, she sure is that."

The day was passing slowly for Sheriff Sam Sinrod. It seemed as if someone had poured molasses into the works of the oak Regulator clock on the wall. Being shaken awake at an ungodly hour always did make him tired. Sam had drunk another half-dozen cups of strong coffee and smoked two more cigars yet the sluggish hands on the clock showed it to be only eleven-thirty in the morning.

Normally at this time he would be anticipating going to lunch, but he felt stuffed from breakfast. Also the stench of burnt human flesh still clung to the insides of his nostrils as if bits of fried carrion had become lodged there. The foul odor seemed to permeate both his skin and his clothing. Last night Sam had taken two long baths and, although he could not afford to do so, burned the uniform he had worn when Sister Ignacia went up in flames. This was foolishness he realized. Only time was capable of cleansing away such a horrible mix of stench and memories.

Sam heard the phone ring outside of the reception desk, but paid it no mind. Every day in the Grant County sheriff's office brought a procession of family disputes, straying cattle, barking dogs or any number of minor problems that were handled by his deputies. Silver City was usually a nice, quiet, law-abiding town. Or at least it had been until recently.

A tight knot formed in the sheriff's stomach when he saw the tension on Burke Martin's face when the deputy swung the door open.

"We could have another one of those spontaneous human combustion things, Sam," Burke gasped, exhausted from the short run. "Mrs. Amanda Pegler, the wife of that Prophet fellow who burnt up in Dub's Place, called. She was sobbing something terrible, she said her car wouldn't start and that she'd run to the neighbors to use the phone."

"What did she say?" Sam Sinrod bolted up, his fatigue having fled in the blink of an eye.

"Mrs. Pegler says she's in bad need of help, that her eight-year-old boy . . . I think she said his name's Benny . . . was burning up and liable to catch fire, or something like that."

"Well, is the kid on fire or not?" Sam boomed angrily.

"I think she did say something about a fever but I ain't sure, she was terrible upset about—"

Burke Martin never got to finish his words before Sam Sinrod elbowed him aside in a rush to get to the sheriff's cruiser.

Chapter Thirty-Seven

Dr. Whitlock grabbed up the large scuffed leather medical bag he had used for house calls before becoming the county coroner. His eyes were narrow from tension. "Did you just tell me a little boy was on fire?"

"No, Doc," Sam Sinrod answered tersely. "All I know for sure is that the Prophet's widow needs our help *now.*"

"You mean, Amanda Pegler, the wife of the guy who burned up in Dub's Place?"

"Yep, she has two boys to raise. Burke said she called and was terribly upset about the youngest one being 'on fire' or some such thing. I only hope it doesn't turn out to be another case of spontaneous human combustion. That family has suffered enough grief." He nodded to the door. "Let's roll."

"You're in *my* way," Dr. Whitlock said hoisting the heavy bag.

"It's about a five-mile drive out there on a rough gravel road," Sam said, after flipping on the emergency lights atop his cruiser. "I sure hope these old tires will hold out."

"Most all rubber comes out of the East Indies or Malaysia," Whitlock said after lighting a fresh Chesterfield. "When the Japs took over that part of the world it cut off our supply and really put a crimp in driving. There simply isn't any rubber to make new tires out of these days. And the military needs what there are worse than we do."

The sheriff mumbled an answer, but the strident wailing of

the siren drowned his reply.

Less than a mile from town, almost to the Lordsburg highway intersection, the right front tire blew out with a resounding bang.

"Damn it, I just knew this would happen!" Sam shouted, skidding to a stop well off the main road. He turned off the siren and killed the engine to save gasoline. "Let's get that tire changed as quick as we can. Even Vern Jensen isn't likely to be able to patch that one."

"There's nothing but shreds left," Whitlock commented after the dust had cleared and he'd jumped out to investigate. "You grab the jack, I'll loosen the lug nuts."

"Oh dear Jesus," Sam moaned in despair, his head inside the open trunk. "The spare tire's flat!"

"Well, this just keeps getting better and better." The doctor looked up the road. "There's someone coming this way, let's flag them down and ask if they'll drive us out there."

"I don't intend to give whoever it is any choice in the matter," Sam Sinrod said, slamming the trunk closed. "This is an emergency and I *am* the law."

The sheriff came to the doctor's side where they both squinted against the bright sunlight to see who was approaching. After a moment they could make out a rusty old Chevrolet pickup that was coming their way so slowly it barely kicked up any dust.

Sam's tight features relaxed when he recognized the truck. "Thank goodness, that's Payatt Hae, Frank's grandpa. He won't hesitate to help us."

"Yeah," Whitlock said with a nod. "I've met him a few times. He seems like a nice guy but he sure doesn't have much to say, does he?"

"Apaches generally don't waste a lot of breath talking. I can't see where that's a failing."

"Oh I really don't mind quiet folks. Most of my patients these days are quiet as you can get. They're actually rather boring, all considered."

Sam gave a deep sigh then stepped onto the main road waving his right hand. The brakes on Payatt's battered pickup squalled like a banshee as the truck slowed to a stop alongside the disabled cruiser.

The wizened old Indian stared through the open passenger-side window at the cruiser. "You have had a tire go flat," he said simply. "You need to change it."

"Mr. Hae," Sam said with a tone of urgency in his voice, "the spare tire's flat and there's a little boy a few miles out on the road to Lordsburg who's terribly sick. We need to get the doctor to him right away."

"I will drive you there," Payatt said without hesitation. He turned to Chepi. "You must ride in the back to make room for our guests." Dutifully, Chepi opened the passenger-side door and climbed out.

"We'll be happy to ride in the bed," Dr. Whitlock said as he grabbed his case from the cruiser.

"Thank you, Mr. Hae," the sheriff said, helping Chepi into the open pickup bed. "The doctor and I appreciate your help and your hospitality."

Sam Sinrod shot the coroner a firm look that this was not a good time to debate the merits of Apache folkways. Whitlock jumped into the cab, cradled the medical bag in his lap and scooted close to Payatt as the sheriff climbed in.

"I'll tell you when we get to the Peglers' house," Sam said.

Payatt put the truck in gear with a grinding of gears, swung around and began plodding south on the Lordsburg highway. It was quite apparent the old Indian was not going to drive much faster than a man could run.

"We need to get there in a hurry," the sheriff said, glaring at Payatt.

The old Apache paid him no mind. "You have ruined two tires in but a little distance. Mine are not flat. I am driving."

Sam and the coroner exchanged troubled glances. Old Payatt's logic was inescapable, though exasperating. Rushing would likely only accomplish blowing out yet another tire which would delay them even more. Both silently acknowledged this fact by saying nothing while Payatt drove them to their destination at a leaden twenty miles per hour.

When they pulled into the driveway leading to the pallid gray home of the widow Pegler and her two sons, Sam Sinrod felt a burning sensation in his throat when he saw that lonesome tire swing dangling from weathered poles swinging in the hot wind like a broken promise.

A dust devil was swirling dirt and debris across the stark open porch as Payatt's Chevrolet sputtered to a halt. Amanda Pegler threw open the door and ran outside, her curly blond hair being whipped about by the departing whirlwind.

"Thank God!" Amanda's words came as raspy sobs, her reddened, teary eyes focused on the coroner. "Dr. Whitlock, I'm so glad you're finally here. I didn't know what to do when the car wouldn't start. My darling little Benny's burning up with fever and now he's having trouble breathing."

"Show me to him," the doctor said as he jumped from the pickup carrying his medical bag.

Inside the neatly kept house, the slight form of Benny Pegler lay on a sofa in the front room, a small circular fan on a coffee table rustled the white sheet that covered the boy as it played torrid air across him. Above the constant whir of the electric fan could be heard the little boy's sporadic gurgling that crushed Sam Sinrod's spirits to a new level of despair.

"I'm terribly sorry it took us so long to get here, ma'am," the sheriff said, placing a comforting hand on Amanda's shoulder. "It's this damn war. We blew out one tire and the spare was flat. Mr. Hae and his wife came along and were kind enough to drive us."

Amanda gave a tearful nod to the old couple that stood stoically near the open door, then turned her attention to Dr. Whitlock who was examining her stricken son.

"This isn't spontaneous human combustion," Whitlock said without looking away from the sandy-haired boy who, with the sheet removed, appeared as gray as the outside of the house. "I'm thinking it's more of a reaction to a bite of some kind."

Dr. Whitlock turned to Amanda. "Did your son mention anything like that happening?"

A flicker of apprehension crossed her tense features. "Yes, now that you brought it up, Benny mentioned something stung him when he was in the outhouse, but it happened in a 'bad place,' and he refused to show me. It was quite a while after that before he got sick." She gasped. "Oh my God, I should have known. It's a spider. A black widow spider must have bit him. We've killed a lot of them under the seat."

"Sam," Whitlock said, "I want you to find a fruit jar and take it to the outhouse. Be careful, but if there's a spider under the seat, bring it in so I can see for certain what it is." He swallowed hard. "The little boy's testicles are swollen to the size of coffee cups. There's no doubt in my mind he's been bitten by something poisonous. I have to know what it was."

Scant moments later the sheriff returned carrying a pint mason jar. "It is a black widow spider all right. A big one, too—" Sam's voice trailed off when he saw Payatt, Chepi and the doctor were circled about Amanda Pegler, a look of agonized defeat and sorrow were deeply etched in everyone's face. The gray form of eight-year-old Benny was still and silent as stone.

Dr. Whitlock broke the heavy silence. "It was a cardiac arrest, he went fast. There was nothing anyone could do. I honestly don't know if I could have saved him if we had gotten him to the hospital an hour ago. Adults almost never die from black widow spider bites, but children . . ."

Sam Sinrod's throat felt as if it were on fire when he said, "I'm sorry, ma'am." He cocked his head. "Uh, Mrs. Pegler, where is your other boy?"

Amanda stared at him blankly. "Leon is at my mother's in Kansas City. He is twelve years old, big enough to ride a bus by himself. When the money finally comes in from Phil's life insurance, Benny and I were going there too, try and start over. It was all I could afford, sending Leon."

"We're so sorry," Dr. Whitlock said, pulling up the sheet to cover the slight corpse. The death of any child saddened him beyond measure.

Amanda's eyes sparked like blue ice. "I didn't know God could be so cruel. A spider killed my husband. Now another one has gone and killed my little boy."

Payatt Hae spoke for the first time since they had entered the house. "Any god can be troublesome and hard to understand. But it is a fact that all who pass into the Spirit World go to a better place."

Amanda's demeanor hardened. "I'm not sure, Mr. Hae, if Hell wouldn't be a better place than here."

"Uh, Mrs. Pegler," Dr. Whitlock said. "I can send Mr. Thornton, the undertaker, for the body."

"Please take Benny with you. I can't afford the money that would cost. Anton Giem, the rancher whose phone I used, said he would come over and get my car running later today. Tell the mortician I'll be in to make arrangements. Until my husband's life-insurance check comes, all the money I have in this world amounts to less than twenty dollars."

"We will deliver him to the undertaker's, Mrs. Pegler," Sam said firmly. "Would you like for us to send someone out to stay with you?"

"No, I prefer to be alone," Amanda said. "It's something I'll need to get used to."

"I understand," Sam answered.

Amanda Pegler stared through the open doorway into the blazing brightness of a cloudless afternoon. "There is one thing you can do for me, Sheriff."

"Name it."

"Kill that damn spider."

"Yes, ma'am, gladly," Sam said as he went to help Dr. Whitlock wrap the dead body of her son in a sheet.

Later, when Payatt Hae, Chepi, Sam and the coroner began the drive back to Silver City with Benny's sheet-wrapped body in the bed of the pickup, another dust devil hit the swing, sending the black tire swaying playfully, as if a child was in it.

Every eye present noted the event, but not a word was uttered. Sometimes, there really was nothing to say. The parching, lonesome wind that hooted and moaned through the eaves of Amanda Pegler's drab home that sat on a barren flat of dry desert said all that was necessary.

Chapter Thirty-Eight

A tangerine moon was hanging low on a darkening horizon when Dr. Whitlock and Sheriff Sinrod climbed from the coroner's sleek 1940 Cadillac V-16 automobile to stand in front of Archie's Tropicana Cocktail Lounge.

"We should have driven my car today," Dr. Whitlock commented. "I can get a new set of tires when I need them, it's just that I don't feel right about asking for them. The Army has more pressing needs for rubber than I do. If we don't win this war, nothing much will matter."

"Doc," Sam's voice was compassionate. "That boy died only minutes after we got there. You said yourself it wouldn't have mattered even if we had gotten him to the hospital."

"Yes, I know. Days like this one are just hard to take is all. Any death is hard, but children are the absolute worst to endure."

"Well, let's have a beer and try to think of something cheery, maybe Sergeant Black's turned into a pile of ash by now."

Dr. Whitlock shook the last Chesterfield from a gold case and lit it. "Naw, we couldn't be that lucky." He gave a jaundiced look at the brown palm trees alongside the entranceway. "I wish Archie would get rid of those dead palms, they're downright depressing."

Sam's thin moustache curled up slightly in a mischievous grin. "Those trees are simply dormant, they'll green up when the mood strikes them. Quit being such a old fusspot. Any coroner who gets in a funk over dead trees is worthless as a glassblower with hiccups."

Dr. Whitlock gave a snorting laugh. It felt good to smile again. "Sherlock, you are just what the doctor ordered. Let's go grab a booth then you can do one other thing to improve my attitude."

"And that would be buy you a drink or I'll miss my best guess."

"Yep," Whitlock said heading for the doorway. "Shucks, that sounds so good, I think I'll let you buy me two."

Sam Sinrod drained the bottle of Carling Black Label beer of its last golden drop and added it to a growing profusion of empties at the end of their booth. He kept trying to think of something that might raise his friend's spirits, but after yet another disaster striking, the task had become a daunting one.

"I still can't believe Kathy Webster running off and getting married like she did." The coroner twirled his nearly empty bottle worriedly on the scarred wood top. "I really was planning to ask her out. She was one cute chick, and a tad flat-chested, but she had nice gams."

Sam said, "We *have* had some rather burning issues to deal with lately that took up a lot of your time."

The coroner's face remained granite-like. "What's hard to believe is her marrying Vern Jensen, the mechanic at the county garage. He's older than sin. I'm betting he's at least fifty. And he's too fat to be healthy."

"She married him mighty quick, too. I think Kathy Webster must have been a lot more desperate for a wedding ring on her finger than we'd supposed."

Dr. Whitlock finished his beer and motioned to Archie's new waitress to bring them another round. "Well, Sam, I suppose it could be for the best, this Mattie Bloom has a lot better figure."

"She sure is bigger in the right places. And Mattie's eyes are normal sized, too. Kathy always looked like she'd been goosed."

"Yeah, onward and forward." The coroner cocked his head in puzzlement. "Or something like that, anyway."

"You ought to not waste any time with this one. The Copper Dome Theater is showing *Stagecoach* this weekend, maybe she'd like to see it with you."

"I hear that's a John Wayne movie where a lot of folks get killed off on a stage heading to Lordsburg. I wonder if it's based on a true story?"

The sheriff shrugged. "At least it saved 'em from having to eat a meal in that town. Being tortured by Indians is preferable to suffering from food poisoning in some restaurant there."

"Here you go, boys." Mattie Bloom's silken voice was akin to an invitation to Heaven. She flashed emerald eyes at Dr. Whitlock and winked when she set the drinks on the table. "Two ice-cold Carling Black Labels. That'll be thirty cents cheap."

The coroner grinned and tossed a silver half-dollar onto her drink tray. "Keep it, toots." He admired the way her glistening raven hair cascaded to her shoulders like a waterfall at midnight. The young lady had also unbuttoned the upper three buttons of her tight-fitting red blouse, which drew his attention to the most excellent cleavage he had seen since Penelope Leathers. A faint mewing sound coming from the other side of the booth indicated the sheriff had also taken note of Mattie's considerable endowments.

"I'm from Iowa," Mattie volunteered. She seemed in no hurry to wait on other customers. "A town called Waterloo. This is my first time away from home. I think the mountains here are so beautiful. I simply love them."

"Mountains are nice," Dr. Whitlock said as he forced himself to tear his gaze from the waitress's exceptional bosom. "With you being new in town I would love to show you about. Perhaps I could take you to a movie this coming weekend, say Saturday.

My name is Bryce, by the way, Bryce Whitlock."

"Oh I know who you are, Doctor. Archie and lots of the other customers have told me all about you." She turned to Sam Sinrod, smiled and bent close, sending him scrunching into the woodwork. "And you are cute Sheriff Sinrod who is awfully shy around girls." Mattie stroked a velvet hand along Sam's startled and suddenly crimson face. "There's no need to be; all us girls want is to make you happy."

The sheriff answered with a watery gurgle that reminded Dr. Whitlock of the last sound he heard from a patient before calling the undertaker.

"Our sheriff's improving, Miss Bloom," the doctor said. "A few months ago the shock of that would've killed him." Whitlock tapped a cigarette from his restocked gold case and offered it to her.

Mattie leaned over to allow Whitlock to light the Chesterfield. Her velvet voice was sensuous, promising, "I look forward to the movie and getting to know you better, Dr. Whitlock."

"Please, call me Bryce."

"I will be counting the hours, Bryce." Mattie turned and flowed away with the silence and grace of a cloud, leaving behind the lingering aroma of spring roses.

The coroner turned to his thunderstruck friend. "Take a few deep breaths. Then the nice widdle sheriff will feel all better."

Sam Sinrod gasped and took a long swallow of beer. "We have *got* to come here more often. I don't know if Mattie's a vamp or so green she doesn't know that she just came across like one."

Whitlock gave a deep sigh. "It looks like the task of finding out has fallen on my shoulders. I'll do my best and give you a report Monday."

The sheriff grinned thinly. "And I'm thinking the good doctor might just have met his waterloo."

When Sheriff Sinrod and the coroner left the cocktail lounge, a full moon was hanging high and orange in a jeweled canopy of twinkling stars. Not a single cloud marred Heaven's light show.

Both were in a buoyant mood until they turned in unison to survey the dead palm trees that stood like corpses on both sides of the doorway. The men exchanged somber glances, then without a single word, they climbed into Dr. Whitlock's Cadillac and drove away into the stifling hot night.

Chapter Thirty-Nine

Burke Martin was having a most excellent dream. A feisty, beautiful redhead who he remembered from a long-ago romp in Madame Millie's place, had just become quite athletic when the sound of distant screams intruded on his pleasure.

The deputy tried to sort out his jumbled thoughts. Being jolted from sleep always left him confused. He finally remembered he was on jail duty, a boring job if there ever was one.

From the angle the sun was shooting through the windows, he realized it wasn't yet past noon. *But who was screaming?* Burke's brain cells began to line up, *the only prisoner we have is Fred Dickerson, and he's a regular. If that guy wasn't forced to sober up in jail once in a while, he'd burn out his liver for sure.*

Yet the guttural screaming continued. It was akin to the death cry of some mindless animal. *Fred Dickerson had no reason to scream.*

Burke Martin jumped to his feet just as the wailing ceased. He grabbed the ring of keys from his belt, fumbled and dropped them. It was when he recovered the keys to the cellblock and stood that he smelled the sickly sweet and unmistakable aroma of burning human flesh.

"Oh my God!" the deputy was met with a cloud of smoke as he swung open the steel door that entered the corridor of cells. "We've got another one."

"This is getting downright repetitive," Dr. Whitlock smeared a generous helping of camphor across his upper lip. "Being in a close space like a jail cell makes the smell even worse."

Sam Sinrod reached over and borrowed the green bottle. He applied a healthy finger full below his nose before replying, "I can't blame Burke any for having to go upchuck his cookies. If people don't stop doing this sort of thing around here, I'm quitting my job and moving to Montana."

"We can drive there together," the coroner said, cocking his head to examine the still-smoking pile of ashes on the floor of the shadowy jail cell. "I've never heard of people catching on fire all by themselves in Montana, likely too cold for it to happen there."

"I wish someone would come up with a reason this is happening *here*." Sam wiped at a leaky eye. "After that poor nun burned up, I had hopes that would be the last of them. Then possibly the reporters would leave me be. Those people are becoming really pesty to deal with."

"They smell a story."

"Sure wish that was all I smelled," Sam Sinrod turned a key in the lock. The cell door opened without the expected squeak. "Someone must have oiled the hinges. That was something that needed doing."

"You should've heard all the screaming he did." A pale Burke Martin came clumping toward them down the narrow stone corridor. "It was terrible to endure."

"I find that interesting," Dr. Whitlock said. "No one heard a peep out of any of the others. Of course, Percy Guttman could have yelled his head off, so he might not have gone quietly into that good night. But screaming indicates extreme pain."

"All of them wound up not requiring Barth to work up a sweat burying them," Sam said. "What is your point?"

"I'm forming a disquieting theory." The coroner rubbed his brow worriedly. "We are dealing with a totally unknown agent here. One that is transmitted in an unknown manner, but most likely by water or air. If this agent is an organic substance such as germs or a virus, it could be mutating from its original form; becoming something entirely new."

"Sort of like the flu," Sam Sinrod added with a degree of understanding that surprised the doctor. "The Spanish flu killed millions only to disappear completely. If the flu can change how it attacks a person, so might spontaneous human combustion."

Dr. Whitlock nodded in agreement. "The cause, whatever the hell it is, could have mutated to where extreme pain accompanies the onset." He took out his gold cigarette case, stared at it a moment, then slid it back into his jacket pocket. "We don't have a clue what the parameters for this disease are . . . but from what I've seen so far I believe it could be a disease. If this agent is easily spread and mutates to be non-selective as to what causes it to immolate the subject, we could be looking at the extinction of the entire human race."

"Well, aren't we in a cheery mood today," Sam said with a frown. "I think you really need to get out of the morgue more often."

"You mean we might all burn up?" Burke Martin's eyes were wide with fear.

Dr. Whitlock turned to the distraught deputy. "You can calm down. I only voiced a theory. We would surely cause a panic if any of what you overheard gets out. And for all I know, there may not be any germ causing this, or no mutations occurring."

"He means he wants you to keep your trap shut," the sheriff added sternly. "And I'm plain telling you to do it. Besides, like the Doc said, we don't know but what this will all blow over. It may easily turn out to be something we can take care of."

"Six people have burnt up," Burke Martin said. "I'd venture we need to get a tad more efficient, but don't worry, I won't say anything about it maybe spreading. A panic isn't anything we want to deal with."

"Thanks, Burke," Sam said. "Now, let's sweep up the remains and air the place out." He hesitated. "And if Fred Dickerson had any family, we need to notify them of his demise."

"I looked at his file while I was, uh . . . out." Burke Martin shuffled his feet nervously. "That was when I remembered Fred Dickerson had a twin brother who lives east of town past the cemetery. Up until a few minutes ago you couldn't have told them apart. They were identical twins right down to their haircuts. Joe is his brother's name. Fred was the problem. That man loved his whiskey in the worst way. He'd forget to eat and his liver was getting to be bigger than the rest of him put together."

"Cirrhosis of the liver," Dr. Whitlock said with a tone of sadness. "That is simply scar-tissue buildup. Too much alcohol without some food to help the liver absorb it will eventually kill a person."

"That's why we tossed him in jail once in a while," Sam said. "We were only trying to be good to him."

Burke Martin continued, "Now Fred's brother wasn't like that at all. He is not only a teetotaler, but he's a deacon in the First Baptist Church. If I recollect correctly, his wife took off on him back in thirty-nine, left town with a furniture deliveryman from Lehman's Department Store. Last I heard, Joe hadn't spent any time or money trying to get her back. I'd reckon he was glad to see her gone. That woman was probably hard to live with as Hester Guttman. Her cousin, Sally, was married for a while to my brother Willie. Now those two fought—"

"We were talking about notifying the deceased's brother," Sam interrupted. If someone asked Burke Martin what time it was, he would proceed to tell them how to build a watch. "I think we should do that."

"That's the odd part," Burke looked concerned. "I'm sure

Joe still works nights at the copper mill over in Santa Rita, that means he sleeps days. When I was in the office getting some fresh air, I tried calling him. Joe Dickerson has a phone you know. Well sir, I let that thing ring itself off the wall, but never did get an answer. I think that's strange, that man should have been there."

Sam Sinrod and Dr. Whitlock looked at each other.

"Oh shit," they said in unison.

Chapter Forty

"A quick pull on the chain would save the county paying the undertaker for another easy burial," Sam Sinrod observed as he, Dr. Whitlock and Burke Martin stood in the small confines of Joe Dickerson's bathroom staring at the layer of black ashes floating in the toilet.

"That *was* considerate of him to burn up while sitting on the john," Dr. Whitlock said. "But look at the seat, it doesn't even have the paint blistered on it. And those house shoes he was wearing have ashes inside them from where his feet were consumed, yet the shoes themselves appear to be totally undamaged. This is strange and a lot different from the others."

"What are you getting at?" Deputy Martin asked, wishing he had rubbed some camphor under his nose when he had the opportunity. At least this scene of spontaneous human combustion had time to air out somewhat before they got here.

"The heat on this victim became focused internally more so than the rest of the cases we've seen." The coroner picked up a slipper, dumped the ashes into a wastebasket and examined it closely. "Remember, the Prophet generated so much heat he burned through a barroom floor. The banjo player melted his way through the bed of a truck. This shoe should have burned up, but it didn't."

"Perhaps sitting over water like he was kept him cooler," the sheriff said hopefully. "I wouldn't want to think this disease, or whatever the hell it is, could be mutating like you were saying it might, Doc."

Burke Martin took a step back, then shrugged his shoulders with obvious indifference. "I reckon this is something like catching a cold; not much a person can do about the situation."

"Unfortunately you may be correct," Dr. Whitlock said. "But so far no one who has had contact with any of the victims have fired off. That's what makes this whole rash of people burning up so puzzling. There has been no common thread to connect any of the cases, until now."

"Fred Dickerson burned up in my jail cell," Sam Sinrod said. "The ashes floating in that toilet belong to his brother, Joe."

"His *identical twin* brother," the coroner added.

"Well, now we know why he didn't answer his phone," Burke Martin commented, drawing stares from his companions. Sometimes the chubby deputy had difficulty staying with a train of thought.

Dr. Whitlock continued, "Twins are actually rare occurrences in the human species. Identical pairs are even more so. In all of our cases of spontaneous human combustion, this is the first time we have had any dots to connect. Twins burning up on the opposite sides of town at about the same time can't be a coincidence."

Sam Sinrod blinked, then reached down and grabbed up a wristwatch he had just noticed laying next to the wall, fairly well covered with ashes. "This is a Longines just like mine. They're really dependable." He held it up, frowned and gave it a thump. "This one seems to have stopped."

"Heat likely destroyed the temper in the mainspring," Dr. Whitlock said. "This immolation might not have been such a cool one after all."

The sheriff turned to Burke Martin. "What time was it when you heard the screaming coming from the cell?"

The deputy rolled his tongue along his cheek. Telling the sheriff he had been asleep at the time wasn't a good idea. "I didn't take notice until I'd run back and checked out the situation and then called you. That must have taken me five minutes at most. When I hung up the phone it was eleven thirty-five."

Sam Sinrod stared at the watch in his hand. "This stopped at eleven forty-five exactly. That means they fired off ten minutes apart." He shook his head in puzzlement. "This sort of shoots holes in the theory of identical twins burning up at the exact same time."

Dr. Whitlock gave a worried sigh, "The jail is what, maybe four, five miles to the west of here?"

"Yeah," Burke Martin answered. "That would be about right. So what?"

"And what direction was the wind blowing from?"

"Sweet Jesus," Sam Sinrod said, his eyes wide. "The wind always blows from the west. Whatever we are dealing with is airborne. It took the ten minutes for the wind to carry whatever the hell this is, the distance from the jail to here."

The coroner nodded in agreement. "Remember, there must be a thousand people living in that big of an area. Yet no one but an identical twin went up in smoke. At least that we know of. This whole mess just keeps getting stranger and stranger."

"And if we don't stop these people from burning up, we can kiss our jobs goodbye," Sam Sinrod said.

"I'm glad I'm just a deputy," Burke Martin said. "That's a safe job to have in times like these."

"It is obvious that only a few people are susceptible to whatever agent is causing this." Dr. Whitlock turned to stare at the ashes floating in the toilet. "Let's just pray it either stays that way or stops altogether."

"This plague blew in from California," Burke Martin said worriedly. "Maybe a Jap submarine surfaced off the coast of

California and released a jar of spontaneous human combustion germs into the air. Those gooks wouldn't think anything of doing something like, not after they snuck up on us at Pearl Harbor like they did."

Dr. Whitlock led the way back outside so they could be away from the all-too-familiar stench. He took a moment to light up a Chesterfield before saying anything. "Deputy Martin might actually be on to something. Germ warfare is a terrible scenario to consider, but with a war going on, it's a distinct possibility."

"The Germans used poison gas in the first war," Sam said. "I don't see a lot of difference between gas and germs, they both kill women and children the same as soldiers. It's a dirty way to fight a war."

The doctor watched a buzzard circling overhead. "There is no such thing as a good war. Killing people by the millions is insanity."

"They started it," Burke Martin said testily.

"Yeah," the coroner said, keeping his gaze to the sky. "That's always the way a war begins."

Sam Sinrod motioned to his deputy. "Grab the camera and we'll photograph the scene, then gather up the remains. When we get back to the office I'll get on the phone to some of the other sheriff departments to the west, Tucson, Yuma and San Diego. If I just ask if they have had any unexplained deaths by fire I expect I won't sound too foolish."

"That's a good idea." Dr. Whitlock appeared worried. "Let me know what you find out." He hesitated. "Uh, Sam, you really aren't going to flush that toilet, are you?"

The sheriff gave only a mischievous grin as he turned to go back inside of the house.

Mattie Bloom set a pair of sweaty bottles of Carling Black Label beer in front of Dr. Whitlock and Sam Sinrod. "You boys look like you're in a funk. Maybe these will cheer you up."

"Things are improving already," the doctor said casting a furtive glance to Mattie's cleavage which was more exposed than usual. "I am looking forward to Saturday."

"Er, er, er," Sam murmured.

"Gotta run," Mattie spun to leave. Every eye in Archie's lounge followed her jiggling departure.

The sheriff took a healthy swallow of beer. "Now that woman is one slick chick."

"And so is Tina."

"Tina doesn't show it off like Mattie does. Mae West isn't as hot."

Dr. Whitlock rolled his untouched bottle of beer around the top of the scarred booth. "So you didn't find any other cases of spontaneous human combustion?"

"No, Doc, like I told you, everyone I talked to acted like they didn't know what I was talking about." Sam took another swallow. "It would be good to be a sheriff where people had the courtesy to die like they are supposed to."

"You're right there. I called Dr. Rogers today, but he was out. I'm hoping he can shed some light on these cases. All I seem to be doing is coming up with more questions."

"Hey," the sheriff said happily, "we got through today with only two voters going up in flames on us. Cheer up, drink your beer and think of Mattie."

"You should have been a doctor." The coroner picked up his bottle. "Because that is the best prescription I know of."

CHAPTER FORTY-ONE

Sam Sinrod could not help but wonder why Dr. Whitlock had phoned and left a message requesting him to drop by his office. He did not mind however. The coroner's underground morgue was always pleasantly cool. That would help make the visit more palatable. The worst part of visiting the morgue was the collection of grisly distractions his friend kept in glass jars that seemed to be everywhere. Many of them were hard to keep from worrying over, or forget about.

The parching heat of this strange year had built to its zenith. Even the oldest denizens of Silver City had never seen the mercury in the thermometer on the sign protruding from Grant County's three-story First National Bank building indicate one hundred and seven degrees before. And the hottest part of the day had yet to arrive.

When the sheriff stepped out into the blazing sun, the torrid air felt thick, almost oily. He realized there was not a hint of breeze, something nearly unheard of here in the foothills of towering mountain peaks. Not a single dog could be heard barking. Even the flies had apparently deemed the weather too hot to buzz about. The silence was as stifling as the terrible heat.

It would not be much of a stretch to envision catching afire right here and now, Sam thought. *Maybe I could simply blame the weather for those people burning up.*

Sam snorted at the folly of his thinking. He really *did* need something concrete to put on the reports, however. Every day brought a fresh rash of phone calls and letters from reporters and other lawmen asking for an update on his progress. So far he had been successful in ignoring all of them, but some were becoming quite determined to have an answer. Dr. Whitlock's theory of spontaneous human combustion possibly spreading was a nightmare he didn't want to come true.

The other problem haunting Sam was that he had not a clue what to tell anyone. On the good side no one else had caught fire since Fred Dickerson and his twin brother had gone up in smoke at pretty much the same time. Maybe his luck would change and there would be no more people burn up.

Perhaps, he thought, *if people quit burning up for no good reason, the matter would quietly go away. With a world war raging, there were other, more important things to focus on than a small town sheriff being plagued by a few oddball immolations.*

Sam smiled at the new set of tires on his cruiser and marveled that Vern Jensen had taken it upon himself to requisition them. Perhaps he could someday forgive the corpulent mechanic for marrying Kathy Webster. This was for Bryce's benefit of course. The good doctor seemed hellbent to get married, while Sam himself was quite content remaining single, for the near future, anyway.

Mattie Bloom was a fresh enigma. She came across as hot enough to ignite matches. Her sexy demeanor made Mae West appear to be a choir girl. Dr. Whitlock, however, seemed perfectly willing and eager to sort the dross from Archie's stable of waitresses.

Sam reminded himself that his friend's track record with women wasn't all that good. John Thayer, over at the pawn shop, would almost certainly raise money for someone to run against the sheriff in the next election if he had to rescue another of Doc's wayward engagement rings. No, he would, on top of everything else going on, be forced to keep a close eye on that girl, for his friend's sake, of course.

To provide enough flat ground to build the magnificent hospital that overlooked Silver City, a crew of miners had blasted away a huge section of mountain. The deepest part of this excavation was set aside as the morgue for good reason; it retained cold like a sponge.

When Sheriff Sinrod opened the door into the windowless hallway that fronted Dr. Whitlock's underground office, the cool air was sweet and welcome as the embrace of a long-lost lover.

"Well, hello, *Sam,*" Tina's unusually familiar and sexy voice shook him from his reverie with a start. "It's so good to see you again."

"Uh . . . hi, Tina, the Doc phoned and asked me to drop by."

The scent of spring rose blossoms grew heavy in the air when Sam approached the secretary's desk. Tina's eyes sparkled like black pearls in an emerald sea of eye shadow. He took note of her trim white uniform, which appeared to be filled out much better than he had previously noted.

"Yes, Sheriff," the nurse's voice came across with a purr. "Both of us are anxious to see you."

"*Both* of you," Sam sputtered hoarsely.

"It is the doctor's idea," Tina's voice purred with promise. "He said he has a date to go to the movies Saturday and thought it would be nice if we made it a double. Dr. Whitlock said you were so busy that you'd likely wait until the last minute to ask me so it would be best for me to mention it first. After all, a girl needs time to get ready."

Tina's brow took on a slightly worried look. Sheriff Sinrod seemed shocked at the prospect of going on a date with her. He also appeared to be having trouble breathing.

"Uh, Sheriff," Tina said softly, "I didn't mean to be too

forward and upset you. Dr. Whitlock thought—"

"Er . . . er . . . er, okay," Sam wheezed. "Er . . . er . . . er, that'll be great."

Tina gave him a sensuous smile. She admired men who pretended to be shy. They were so refreshing to be around compared to the miners she had dated previously. "I'm looking forward to going out with you."

Sam Sinrod bolted past the now-beaming secretary and into the morgue. The ever-present pungent smell of formaldehyde helped bring his mind back into focus.

Dr. Whitlock sat behind his desk smoking a Chesterfield, grinning like a cat with a feather dangling from its mouth. "Tell me, Sherlock, did 'ems actually get a date for a change?"

"Yeah, and thanks for the warning. I'm so darn happy, I'll let you pay."

"If you can speak in complete sentences being in the company of two beautiful girls for the entire evening, I'll be glad to."

"We'll go Dutch treat." Sam took a seat across the desk, his gaze immediately fell on some gruesome photographs of a man with his entire belly laid open.

Dr. Whitlock nodded to the picture. "That was an odd case I had when I was practicing back in Pennsylvania. I'd been poring through everything I could think of concerning people burning up when I ran across this old file I'd kept on Buford, the Fire King. He was a carnival performer."

"Not really very good at his job, I'd say."

"And not overly bright. Buford inhaled propane to be able to shoot flames from his mouth. I would imagine he made a real impression on the audience that night he caught a case of hiccups and sucked flames into his stomach."

Sam shrugged. "You could say he got a bang out of his work." The sheriff slid the pictures away, his features growing serious. "You didn't ask me here to show me pictures of a dead idiot."

"No Sam, I didn't." Dr. Whitlock leaned back in his chair, thoughtfully puffing away at his cigarette. "I was on the telephone with Jim Rogers, the medical examiner in Santa Fe, for over an hour. He took the section of Roan Walker's leg I sent him to that new government laboratory in Los Alamos where they gave him access to what is likely the most powerful microscope in existence."

"What did he find out?"

"You really should light up a cigar, this will take some explaining. While we don't know how it was initiated, we *do* know why those seven people burned up."

Chapter Forty-Two

The shadows across Sam Sinrod's heart fled as he extracted a black Cuban cigar from his shirt pocket. He bit the tip off, wearing a satisfied expression. It was far past time to fill out the paperwork on these strange cases and get back to normal sheriff duties such as sobering up drunks and writing out speeding tickets to the occasional tourist.

"Okay, Dr. Watson," Sam said after firing his cigar using Whitlock's ornate brass desk lighter. "Fill me in on how we can sweep the ashes under the rug, so to speak."

The coroner took time to fill a pair of mugs with Tina's excellent coffee and set them out before returning to his desk and the voluminous handwritten notes next to his phone.

"A lot of this, Sam, is scientific conjecture," Dr. Whitlock said as he thumbed through the stack of paperwork, a studious expression on his face.

"That's what all of you over-educated people call a guess, isn't it?"

"Based on established laws of science, yes. This is rather new territory we're entering here. As I mentioned, we think we've discovered *what* caused these cases of spontaneous human combustion. But not the *how* that initiated the events. That remains a conundrum."

An expression of concerned bewilderment on the sheriff's face caused the coroner to add, "A conundrum means a riddle or puzzle."

"Oh," Sam said with obvious relief. "I knew that."

Dr. Whitlock took a sip of steaming coffee. "I'm going to try and explain this in layman's terms for my benefit as much as yours. As I have mentioned, we are all on a learning curve now.

"To begin to make all of this plain, we need to go to the very basic building blocks of life itself. Let's start with a single cell, which is the structural unit of the body."

"We can do that," Sam took a long thoughtful puff on his cigar. "You forget I *did* go all the way through high school, and studied biology. I remember that while cells differ in function and size, they are comprised of a nucleus and a membrane that holds it together."

The coroner nodded in surprised satisfaction. "I'm quite impressed, Sherlock. Perhaps that 'C' grade average of yours was undeserved. Your understanding of this much biology will help a great deal."

Dr. Whitlock lit a cigarette. He took a long moment to organize his thoughts before continuing. "Now, we need to think even smaller. Cells are the building blocks of all living organisms. To explain what happened to those people who burned up, we have to go to the very building blocks of the cell itself."

"You must mean the nucleus."

"Inside the nucleus, to be precise. That is why Dr. Rogers went to Los Alamos to use what is most likely one of the most powerful microscopes ever built."

"Go ahead, this is becoming interesting, especially what's inside of a tiny cell."

Whitlock's brow lowered in concentration. "Think of the nucleus as the control center of the cell. Within the nucleus we find nucleotides, or what scientists are calling DNA, to save using words big enough to choke on. Liken this DNA to a long rope ladder that is twisted into a spiral shape. By a complicated process we are only beginning to understand, DNA regulates every activity of the cell and hence the entire living organism."

Sam Sinrod shook ash from his cigar into a crystal ashtray. "I may be going out on a limb here, but if I'm following you, what you're getting at here is something strange has come along to influence the DNA."

Dr. Whitlock nodded in honest astonishment. "I really must be a better teacher than I'd thought. The DNA tells a cell when to divide. Somehow this process, which is usually quite normal, has gone wild. The cells have apparently become so overloaded with orders to divide again and again that they simply overheat and explode."

"Like the radiator of a car on a long hill on a hot day."

"I would liken it more to an electrical overload. Think sparks, heat and fire, like what you see when a fuse blows. This is exactly what we saw on that nun at St. Mary's and Garret Black's finger. The nice sergeant probably will be okay unless for some reason the signal to his genes got triggered by contact with that burning corpse. The overload to trigger an entire human to go up in flames would work only if the genetic codes match perfectly."

"So, those poor folks who caught fire had their billions and billions of cells go into overload from being ordered to divide at a fantastic rate until they exploded into flames."

"That appears to be exactly what happened. Jim noted complete destruction in most, but not all, of the cells in Officer Walker's leg. Genetics gone wild is the only theory that works. But at least it does not appear to be a disease. This agent, or whatever, will only trigger spontaneous human combustion in people who hold specific markers, which is why the twins burned."

The sheriff clucked his tongue. "There's not enough room under 'cause of death' to fit all of that in. And even if I did, no one would believe it. I really need something more solid to put out to the press other than a theory."

Dr. Whitlock lit another Chesterfield. "The problem is, like I have alluded, we don't have a clue as to what caused the DNA to 'short out' which is as good of a term for what happened as any. Things like this simply don't happen, at least not outside of a laboratory."

"Except in our jurisdiction," Sam grumbled. "We're *so* lucky."

"Yeah," Dr. Whitlock agreed with a nod. "There are a lot more questions than we have answers for. At least, on the good side, this doesn't appear to be anything that will spread to anyone who does not have very specific genetic markers. We know it is reasonable to assume the cause is airborne, so everyone who fit the parameters has likely already been exposed or burned up. But what was the source, where did it come from? Hell, we don't have any idea what *it* is, for Pete's sake."

"I'm betting this is exactly what happened to the junk dealer, Krook, in *Bleak House,*" the sheriff said firmly.

"Charlie Dickens made that one up, Sam. He did write fiction, you know. But fiction is many times based on fact. There are an awful lot of cases of spontaneous human combustion recorded in history." The coroner sighed, "I've just never heard of seven cases in one area over the space of a few days."

"Silver City seems to attract oddball happenings like a magnet," Sam said with a sigh. "Why couldn't this have struck down in Lordsburg?"

Dr. Whitlock bolted upright, his face a mask of contemplation. "You may have hit on something there. I had never thought of magnetism triggering this, Sam, but that might be it. Jim Rogers mentioned that Army experiments bouncing radio waves off things caused them to heat up. Microwaves he called them, but that sounded impractical and pretty farfetched to me."

Sheriff Sinrod gazed at the coroner with a bland half-smile.

"That girl over at Millie's was *plenty* close to Roan Walker when he fired up. How could a magnet be selective as to who catches fire? By all rights she should have burnt up along with him if that was the cause."

Dr. Whitlock gave a worried stare at the stack of notes. "Sam, I told you this is new ground we're treading on. Sometimes, in science, answering questions like we have to answer could take years of study and research."

Sam gave a deep sigh. "For a time there I had hopes that you might actually have come up with something useful. I should have known better. Not only do I have nothing to tell all of the reporters who keep calling, I've developed one helluva headache."

"*That,* I can cure." Whitlock's usual grin returned. "Take two aspirins and call me in the morning."

The sheriff stood, scooted his chair back and shook his head. "Doc, I must say you have one sick mind."

"As a matter of fact, I do," Dr. Whitlock said with an evil grin. He pointed to a row of glass jars on the far wall. "It's in jar 3-A if you'd like to take a closer look at it."

"I can't take the time," Sam said on his way out the door. "I need to go back to the office and study maps of Montana."

Chapter Forty-Three

A shaft of blazing sunlight, shooting past where Sam Sinrod's pet cat, Jasper, had just flipped the window shade away in pursuit of a bug, struck the sheriff full in the eyes, shaking him from a deep and peaceful slumber. He remembered the windows had just been replaced. While they were boarded over, the cracks were big enough to let half of the bugs and flies in Grant County inside.

The sheriff snorted and rubbed sleep from his eyes. He growled at Jasper, "No one needs a cat, except maybe stuffed and placed on a mantel over the fireplace. And that's where you're heading on greased skids if you don't straighten up." Jasper, of course, ignored him to keep batting at the shade.

Sam wasn't really certain how he'd come to have a cat. Two years ago an obviously starving little tabby kitten had followed him into the house when he had gone to get the milk from off the porch. Sam had felt sorry for the little cat, filled a bowl with milk, warming it slightly on the stove first, then set it on the floor along with a few pieces of ham he had found in the Frigidaire. The cat had stuck around ever since.

Jasper was at least able to fend for himself a lot of the time, usually when the weather was agreeable. Other times, like now, with the temperature ungodly hot, the cat refused to leave the house for any reason. He wondered deeply if having an occasional mouse to put up with might be preferable.

Sam realized the folly of his intentions to sleep late. He

climbed from bed, stretched, then looked to the night stand to find the Big Ben alarm clock showed it to be nearly eight.

"All right, Jasper, I know it's time to get out of the sack." The cat gave up his bug chasing to begin purring loudly and rubbing Sam's legs. The sheriff sighed, pulled on a robe and headed for the front door. "Okay, okay, ya furball, I'll get it as quick as I can."

Ed Von Gendren, the milkman for Red Canyon Dairy, left a quart of milk on his porch every morning, except Sunday. This being Wednesday, a half pound of cheese and butter would also be there. Jasper considered a bowl of milk along with a slice of cheese to be the highlight of his cat week, which explained Sam getting woken up before he was ready.

"The milk won't need warming for you this morning," Sam said, heading for the kitchen after rescuing his dairy products from a scorching porch. Once Sheriff Sinrod had settled Jasper down munching on his usual Wednesday treats, he put the coffeepot on the gas range, lit the burner and a cigar with the same match, then sat down at the kitchen table to read the newspaper.

SHERIFF STYMIED BY RASH OF DEATHS, the headline announced in bold, black print. Sam tried to remember if the newspaper had used bigger type when the Japs attacked Pearl Harbor, but doubted they had. He crushed the entire paper into a ball, tossed it at the wastepaper basket and missed.

After a half dozen cups of black coffee and a bowl of oatmeal with sliced bananas, Sam began to feel alive. He shaved, using one of the few luxuries he had allowed himself: an electric Schick dry shaver. The thing had been amazingly expensive at fifteen dollars. Compared to the hazards of dealing with a straight razor, however, it was an absolute bargain.

Sam Sinrod dressed in faded blue jeans and T-shirt, pulled on a ten-year-old pair of cowboy boots, set a battered straw hat on his slicked-back hair to keep away the blazing sun then strode outside to survey his white, wood-frame home set on an acre of nearly flat ground next to Little Walnut Creek.

A quick look past his brown lawn and dying bushes, to where a few trees were struggling to survive along the once cheerfully burbling creek that was now dry as a Baptist tent revival, hammered home the reality of the drought. If they did not get some rain soon, the whole of southwest New Mexico would become an uninhabitable wasteland.

He deliberately avoided looking up at where those two old men had blown away most all of the once green trees that used to grow in that direction. Having those reprobates living a couple of miles away was a relief. It was a miracle they were still alive and all the damage to his house turned out to be minor.

Sam stared at his push lawnmower that had nothing to cut. He decided this would be a good time to sharpen and oil it, anyway. There were always endless chores to be done around a house, most of which he enjoyed. Burke Martin needed the experience of being an acting sheriff and the chubby man was generally competent enough to handle most matters that came up. Actually, if anyone were to run against him come the next election, it would most likely be Burke.

The sheriff had to keep busy and try not to think ahead. Today was not a day he could take off and relax. After lunch he would bathe, slick his hair with Wildroot Cream Oil, then dress in that dismal black suit he dreaded so much having to wear.

At two o'clock he would be sitting in a front pew at the Rimrock Presbyterian Church, attending the somber funeral of eight-year-old Benny Pegler.

Kathy Koehn played the steam pump organ for the service, which was lightly attended. Kathy was the high-school music teacher and the only person in Grant County who knew how to play the complicated, yet stunningly ornate organ that graced the front of the church. The fact that Kathy was a staunch Catholic was overlooked by any Protestant churchgoers desiring good music.

Sam Sinrod sat in the second row of pews between Bryce Whitlock and Barth Thornton. Amanda Pegler sat in the front pew, close to the open white casket that held the body of her dead son. She wore the appropriate black dress; a veil kept anyone from seeing her tears. Next to Amanda, to everyone's surprise, sat Hester Guttman, clutching a Bible in one hand and a song book in the other; tears made glistening lines down her cheeks.

The sheriff wished fervently there were songs other than *Amazing Grace* and *I'll Fly Away* that could be sung at funerals. To his point of view, they made any death seem even sadder. In a world where thousands of lives were being lost each day fighting either the Nazis or the Yellow Horde, the pitiful death of a little boy added an even deeper sense of pain and despair to the occasion.

Silver-haired and wizened, Johnathan Small, the man who had been the local Presbyterian minister since William Howard Taft was president, stood behind the tall walnut pulpit where he gave words of hope and promise. He intoned with a sad voice that there was another world beyond this veil of tears. It was a place of eternal love where nothing and no one ever dies. In Heaven the lambs lay safely down with the lions, and little boys play happily for all time.

Sam Sinrod hoped the old preacher was right. Then, the service was over. Songs had been sung, words had been said. Now it was up to Barth Thornton to carry on the proceedings.

Sam Sinrod and Bryce Whitlock had been asked by Amanda to act as pallbearers. The coffin was plain and sadly small, their burden slight. Moments later they, along with Anton Giem, Norbert Pike and a couple of church members, stood in bright sun behind the hearse.

The heat was stifling. Once the pine coffin had been secured, all were glad to be able to wear their hats once again.

"This is the hottest summer I can remember," the district attorney said, wiping his brow. "We have simply got to get some rain soon."

Sam Sinrod cast a puzzled expression at the undertaker. "Barth, I was surprised to see Hester Guttman here."

Barth Thornton clucked his tongue. "You know that's the darndest thing I've ever seen. She attends every funeral these days. Hester sobs worse than anyone. I hear tell she's even taken to buying a bottle of wine once in a while. It's for sure she hasn't been the same since her husband died."

Norbert Pike said, "All the years they were married, Hester yelled at poor Percy continually. I never would have guessed she even had a heart, let alone one that could be broken."

"She honestly loved him," Dr. Whitlock said. "I find that sad; she never recognized the fact until it was too late."

The assembled men glanced wordlessly from one to another. Nothing else really needed saying. After a moment, they left to make their way to the cemetery beneath a cloudless blue sky.

Chapter Forty-Four

"I hate funerals so darn bad that I've come to the decision I'm not even going to attend my own," Sheriff Sinrod said over a nearly empty bottle of Carling Black Label beer. "They're too depressing."

Dr. Whitlock rolled his bottle around the outline of a heart that was carved deep into the tabletop of their booth at Archie's lounge. He was staring at the initials inside and contemplating the fates of those long-ago lovers.

"Sam," Dr. Whitlock said eventually, keeping his gaze fixed on the heart, "I don't like funerals any more than you do, but when a person deals with death like we are forced to, it's one of the prices we have to pay." He sighed and took a long drink, then set the empty bottle among others next to the wall. "They do have a tendency to put a man into a funk, however, especially when we have to bury a young child."

"Barth Thornton told me he paid Amanda Pegler five hundred dollars for her home." Sam realized the fire had gone out of his cigar and relit it. "That place sits on forty acres of hard land that'll never be worth anything, with the drought the way it is. I would venture no one else would have bought it at any price. Barth added that his funeral costs were part of the deal."

"Thornton has a big heart; he simply felt sorry for her. At least Amanda Pegler can leave now and be with her other son. Silver City holds nothing but bad memories for that lady."

"Mrs. Pegler was on the bus that left for Albuquerque over two hours ago. Burke Martin told me she dropped by the department to thank us before she left."

"She's still a pretty woman, maybe Amanda will find some happiness yet." Sam's brows lowered. "You did kill that spider? I promised her we'd do that."

"It's floating in jar 4-C on a shelf in the morgue. That black widow's body was not as wide as my little fingernail, yet it was big enough to tear hearts apart."

"How about it, boys?" Mattie Bloom's sultry voice came across as a free ticket to the Promised Land, transporting the men from their gloom. "Are you two ready for another round of ice-cold Black Labels?"

"Mattie you are such a sweet-talker," Dr. Whitlock said with his first smile of the evening. "A man would have to work hard at saying no to such a beautiful girl."

A low mewing from across the booth told the coroner that Sam had once again taken note of Mattie's cleavage. The tight black blouse she wore with the top three buttons unfastened covered Mattie's splendid attributes much like a coat of paint. Even Dr. Whitlock had a difficult time keeping his words straight when she was close. As a pinup girl Mattie Bloom would do justice to any wall. Betty Grable didn't have as much to offer.

"They will be coming right up, boys," Mattie glided away in an invisible cloud of rose blossoms, taking the gaze of every man in the bar along with her.

"Er . . . er . . . er," Sam finally found his voice. "You know if Eve looked that tempting when she set out peddling apples, I don't blame Adam in the least for eating one."

"Yeah, I agree." Whitlock watched until the waitress was out of sight before returning his attention to his friend. "Actually that whole biblical scenario was sort of dumb, if you think about it."

"Why's that?"

"I mean we *are* dealing with the Almighty here. God makes a really big deal out of telling those nice young folks to leave the apples alone, yet he doesn't bother to build a fence around the tree. I mean he doesn't even put up a 'don't eat' sign or anything. It was like he meant for that to happen. And we're dealing with the same God here who made cats. He had to know something about curiosity."

"It does sound like a set-up to me, but why?"

"Ineffable is the word preachers use to describe such goings-on. The big word means that the plan is too deep for us mere mortals to understand."

"I'd think getting kicked out of paradise for just eating an apple is rather harsh punishment for doing something they didn't understand. And they had no jury trial, not even a lawyer."

"You have to go to Hell to find a lawyer, that place is full of them."

Mattie floated to their booth, bent over and set out the beers. "I am really looking forward to Saturday, Bryce." She smiled at the sheriff. "And a double date sounds like *so* much fun."

"Er, yes it does," Sam Sinrod surprised both of them by being able to speak. He tossed a half-dollar to ring on her drink tray. "Er, I'm looking forward to it and you keeping the change."

Dr. Whitlock beamed. "It seems our good sheriff is improving, I must say." The doctor glanced past her through the smoke-filled room to the front windows. "You're busier than usual tonight."

"Yeah," Mattie agreed, turning to survey the bar. "We've got a lot of soldiers here for some reason. I didn't know there were any Army posts nearby."

"There's not," Whitlock said firmly. "Alamogordo is the closest I know of. And that's an Army Air Corps base."

"Nice bunch of guys," Mattie shot a table full of soldiers a delighted look. "They aren't great tippers, but I'd venture every one of them has asked me out, some twice."

I'm sure they have, Dr. Whitlock thought. "They're probably just with a convoy or such passing through. They'll be gone tomorrow."

"Yeah, then again those men could likely just be on leave, coming up here to the mountains to escape the heat. It's too bad they had to get disappointed," Sam said, surprising them by using two complete sentences.

"Gotta run boys, catch ya later," Mattie's voice pealed like silver bells, then she was gone.

"That is one hot little number," the coroner said. "I wonder if she knows just what a knockout she really is. Wars have broken out over uglier women."

"Let's just hope one doesn't break out here." Sam sighed. "This has been a rough enough of a day without a free-for-all with a bunch of soldiers to put up with."

"I wouldn't fret it too much." Dr. Whitlock looked over the packed bar. "All I see are dozens of burly miners, rough-looking cowboys and trained soldiers, all suffering with squirrel fever. I can't fathom anything going wrong here that our brave widdle Sheriff can't handle with one hand tied behind his back."

"Drink up," Sam grinned thinly, holding up a sweaty brown bottle. "We who are about to get the crap kicked out of us salute you."

"There you go," Dr. Whitlock said, grabbing for his beer. "An optimistic attitude is always the best."

"Well that was a surprise," Dr. Whitlock nodded to the wall clock. "It's ten o'clock and not only is all well, the place is almost empty."

"I'm so glad to still be alive," the sheriff said with obvious relief. "Those soldiers leaving all at once like they did came as a surprise. Then the miners and cowboys mostly drifted off."

"They were drinking to get enough courage to fight. Sometimes boredom is good."

"This is one of those times." Sam held up an empty bottle and motioned for Mattie. "One more and we should leave. Can't have voters of Grant County saying we drink to excess."

Dr. Whitlock surveyed the profusion of empty brown bottles of Carling Black Labels that filled the end of their booth. "One more won't be excess—"

A distant rumble shook the countryside then echoed loudly through the bar.

"That didn't sound like any thunder I've ever heard," Sam Sinrod said, bolting from the booth.

"It can't be thunder," Mattie said, looking through the open windows. "There's not a cloud in the sky."

Another distant blast ripped the night air. This time the sheriff along with everyone in Archie's lounge could see a flash of yellow light on the western horizon.

"That's an explosion of some sort. It's sure as hell not thunder!" Sam exclaimed. "I wonder what those two old coots blew up now."

Another point of light flared in the west. Seconds later, a thunderous boom rolled across the normally quiet desert.

Archie Turnbull came running from behind the bar, a wild look on his face no one had ever seen before.

"They're here! It's finally happened. I was in the last big war," Archie screamed, obviously near panic. "I know a bombing when I'm in one. The damn Japs are attacking Silver City. We're all gonna die!"

Chapter Forty-Five

Payatt Hae was extremely proud of his new headdress made of feathers from the sacred bald eagle. Any Apache knew that a bald eagle had the keenest eyesight of all creatures, even surpassing that of a golden eagle or the swift hawk. He now had what was needed to flatten a bothersome windmill.

The colorful headdress that was held together with the skin of a grizzly bear and studded with turquoise had once belonged to the great chief, Dasoda Hae, or, as the white-eyes called him, Mangas Colorado. While Payatt and Dasoda shared the same surname, there was no lineage he knew of to connect him with that great scourge of the *Pinda-lik-o-yi.*

Mangas Colorado had done a very good job of keeping the white-eyes at bay. It was a terrible shame some soldier, who had undoubtedly garnered the favor of a god, had shot him all those many years ago. If the great chief had not been struck down, Payatt might not be having to deal with a dried-up spring.

Having the same last name could be no accident, however. Payatt Hae knew in his heart that he was kin to the late owner of the headdress that had just been given to him by his cousin, Robert Swiftwater.

All of the gods would certainly recognize the wonderful headdress and appreciate its great powers. This would certainly bring focus to *Usen*'s eyes and cause him to see the plight that windmill was causing to one of The People. Then the hated windmill that had dried up his life-giving spring would, as the white-eyes say, be smashed to smithereens. It would be a humbling lesson for them.

This night was good for dancing a *Gahe*. An Apache moon was coming. The Old Ones believed that if a person was killed, the same conditions would prevail in the next life that were present at their death. Apache warriors never attacked at night except during the light of a full moon. Otherwise their spirit could become lost and wander aimlessly about, unable to find the Great Hunting Grounds in the dark.

Payatt Hae finished the last of his hot chocolate, which was one of the few good things the Apache ever received from the white-eyes. Chepi had already gone to bed. It was nearly ten o'clock and his wife of many summers was undoubtedly still tired from her extravagant shopping spree in Silver City. Many store owners there had been enriched by her visit. At least Chepi had bought another one of those wonderful cans of cocoa made by Mr. Hershey. Now there was a white-eyes The People held no resentment for. If the sugar only lasted. The clerk told them it was rationed like gasoline. Living with a world war was not easy.

Then the old Apache remembered the boy who had been called to the Spirit World. There had been a funeral service for him today. Payatt realized he should have gone because he had been present when the boy's spirit had been set free, but he did not have enough gasoline to feed the truck for two trips to town and many of the groceries Chepi had bought would not have lasted in the heat. All spirits however, needed to be guided on their quest for the Great Land beyond. White men seemed to be unaware of this, which did not surprise him—they were woefully unaware of many things.

Payatt decided to also dance a *Gahe* for the boy and ask a small god to guide him on his journey to see to it that he did not go crazy in his quest for the Great Land.

When Payatt Hae stepped from his adobe home and walked into the night, he had gone only a few feet before his senses told him something was terribly strange.

The air was miserably hot, heavy and oily with no breeze to move it about and afford relief. Overhead the campfires of many gods twinkled. The wonderful Apache moon was rising above jagged mountain peaks. He could see nothing amiss, yet he felt the hairs on the nape of his neck stiffen.

Then Payatt realized there was no sound. It was as if all of nature was holding its breath. Crickets, owls, coyotes, all creatures of darkness had been silenced. Never before had Payatt Hae experienced utter silence.

This could only be accounted for by the presence of the Great *Usen* himself. All of creation was in awe of the celebrated god.

Payatt took the powerful headdress and held it high against the yellow orb of the rising moon, then placed it on his head. It was time to beseech the most powerful of gods to flatten a windmill.

The distant tower of the hated windmill stood against the coming Apache moon like a bony statue. Payatt glared at it with all of the amassed contempt of his ancestors against the *Pinda-lik-o-yi,* then he began to dance a *Gahe.*

Payatt was amazed how little time it took for the *Gahe* to work. He had not completed his second circle and had sung only part of one ritual when the earth quivered beneath his feet like the dying flesh of some great beast.

A towering flower of orange flames bloomed where the hated windmill stood. The venerable old man was forced to shield his eyes from the brightness, but he knew in his heart that windmill had been turned into history. What amazed Payatt was the force *Usen* had taken to demolish it. The *Pinda-lik-o-yi* windmill was not *that* big.

Yet it was good that *Usen* had finally seen fit to answer his entreaties after all this time. A god that continually ignores man is very worthless. "Now," as his grandson would say, "*Usen* is cooking with gas."

Another flash accompanied by an explosion that most certainly blew a window out of his home rattled the desert night. Payatt was knocked to the ground by the concussion. One more flash of blinding light and a final thunderclap gave an end to *Usen*'s fury. Only a wall of flame that gave off towers of smoke was left rolling slowly across the distant hillside, like a wave on water.

Payatt managed to stand on shaky legs. There was no reason for that god to destroy the side of a mountain just to flatten a little windmill. A simple fireball had been all he had asked for. Now he would certainly incur the wrath of the white-eyes. Causing this much fire in such a dry time could not help but spread destruction and cause him grief once they found out about his *Gahe*. Yes, the sheriff would certainly put him in jail for causing his county to burn up.

A deep growl, like a provoked bear in a cave came from the billowing, roily smoke. Payatt stood stone still as the growling grew in intensity, coming closer and closer. There was no doubt in his mind that all of this activity by the gods had attracted some evil spirit. From all of the loud growling coming from the clouds of smoke he had brought out a really *big* evil spirit. This was not good. This was not good at all.

Something huge could definitely be seen coming toward him through the smoke. Payatt Hae knew that he was responsible for this thing being here. He wished fervently that he had paid closer attention to the medicine man when he was telling how to repel evil spirits.

The old Apache straightened his headdress of eagle feathers. *Usen* had finally come through on the windmill. There was no doubt in his mind that only the Great God could stop whatever was headed for him. Another *Gahe* was his only chance. He began to chant and dance. After only a moment, with much roaring, growling and clacking of huge teeth, the monstrous thing came out of the smoke and fire.

Payatt Hae's blood froze when he saw what it was.

Chapter Forty-Six

"I'm betting it's not the Japs like Archie thinks," Sheriff Sinrod yelled over the wailing siren of his cruiser. "The attack might be coming from out of the north. In my book that would mean it's gotta be the Nazis. After the way those yellow rats snuck up on us at Pearl Harbor, I reckon it shouldn't come as any great surprise that the Nazis might try the same kind of sneak attack."

"Archie suffers from shell shock he got from being in the First World War," Dr. Whitlock said. "When a car backfires he has to take a sedative and lay down for a while. All this might turn out to be is an airplane crash."

Sam Sinrod took a worried puff on his cigar. He looked in the rearview mirror and studied the pinpoints of flashing lights of Freeman Bates' pickup and county fire truck that were following them in the distance, then sighed. "You may be on to something. This isn't right, even the craziest Japs won't be wasting bombs on Silver City."

"I was thinking the same thing," Whitlock said tapping a Chesterfield from his cigarette case. "If we were being bombed I can't figure the Japs passing over San Diego and Phoenix just to blow us up."

"And then miss us," Sam added. "The whole town is lit up like a Christmas tree."

"*Something* sure as hell did a good job of blowing up. If half of New Mexico doesn't burn up from this it'll be a miracle."

"The whole countryside is a tinderbox, why we can't see fire heading up the mountainside is a mystery—" The sheriff bit hard on his cigar. "Payatt Hae's place is near whatever blew up. I hope they're all right."

"We'll find out in a minute or two, his house is just over the next rise."

Sheriff Sinrod pushed the accelerator pedal to the floor. Having a new set of tires meant he did not have to lollygag. The speedometer on the Ford Fordor indicated the cruiser was traveling nearly sixty when they shot over the crest of the hill and looked down on Payatt Hae's small ranch.

"Oh Lord and butter!" Sam shouted, as he slammed hard on the brakes.

Chapter Forty-Seven

"You two men get out of that car. Keep your hands where I can see them!" The burly Army MP barking orders was flanked by two wide-eyed young soldiers who kept submachine guns pointed straight at Sam Sinrod and Dr. Whitlock.

"I don't think this would be a really good time to debate military policy," the coroner sputtered, keeping his eyes on the roadblock that had stopped them in front of Payatt Hae's adobe home. "And it appears to me these gentlemen do have the upper hand."

"This is my jurisdiction, dammit," Sheriff Sinrod growled. "They don't have the right to do this."

"When we get back to town I'll help you compose a really nasty letter of complaint," Whitlock said, reaching for the door handle. "Right at this moment however, I feel we're obligated to assist our armed forces by honoring what seems to be a reasonable request."

The sheriff glared through the windshield. "Those soldiers are packing Browning automatic rifles. They're powerful enough to shred this cruiser."

"My point exactly, Sam. Now, I suggest we both proceed really slow and see what these nice men want of us."

Sam Sinrod rolled his cigar angrily in his mouth for a moment, then joined Dr. Whitlock who was already standing outside the cruiser holding his hands high.

The MP, who on closer examination had features that could

have been chiseled from a concrete block, surprised them when he took a folder from a scuffed leather briefcase, stared at Sam and Bryce in the bright lights that illuminated the area from a high tower mounted on a trailer. His eyes flitted between the men and the folder several times.

"You two are Sheriff Sam Sinrod and the Grant County coroner, Dr. Bryce Whitlock." The MP's gravelly voice came across as more of a declaration than a question. "Follow me, please."

"See," Whitlock whispered cheerfully in the sheriff's ear. "He said 'please.' We're beginning to woo them over already."

The MP halted, spun and growled at the two gun-toting soldiers, "When Freeman Bates and the fire trucks arrive, order them back to town. Tell him the Army's got everything under control here." He hesitated. "But be sure to thank them for coming out. We are under orders not to anger the civilians more than we have to."

"Yes sir," came the snappy retorts.

Sam and Bryce were relieved to see there were no longer machine guns pointed at them. At the same time they were puzzled as to how the MP, who seemed to be in charge, knew everyone's names or the fact that any fire trucks were even coming. They wouldn't be appearing over the top of that hill for another few minutes.

The duo turned and began following the still-nameless MP, who was obviously herding them to the general direction of Payatt Hae's backyard. They could not help but be amazed at the scope of what was transpiring on the mountainside where they had earlier found the piece of metal that had struck the earth above the windmill.

Two large bulldozers were peeling away large smoking sections of earth with their blades, leaving glistening rock in their wake. These bulldozers were not like any they had seen before.

Metal cabs enclosed the tracked machines. Small round windows gave the operators a meager view as to what they were pushing around by the light of six light towers powered by rumbling generators. Numerous trucks, jeeps and oddly enough a halftrack, all painted drab olive green, dotted the gentle valley.

"It doesn't look like we have to worry about the fire spreading any," Sam ventured. "But those machines are huge. It took a lot of time and effort to truck those things in here undetected."

Dr. Whitlock only grunted. He took a chocolate bar from his pocket and wolfed it down. *This is one helluva time to have my diabetes act up.*

Momentarily, they walked by Payatt Hae and his wife, Chepi, who were sitting on a bench while stoically watching the bulldozers tear apart the distant mountainside. Both men thought it odd the old Apache had an eagle-feather headdress in his lap, but decided with everything else going on, not to mention it.

At least two dozen uniformed soldiers milled about. All were armed with both rifles and side arms. It was gratifying to note none were pointed at them. Actually, most of the soldiers appeared rather bored. Some were joking, smoking cigarettes, completely ignoring the sheriff and coroner as they followed the MP past them.

To add to the strangeness of this night, Sam Sinrod and Dr. Whitlock were ushered to where a silver-haired man, impeccably dressed in an officer uniform and wearing aviator sunglasses, sat in a chair behind a polished oak desk. There was no building or roof over it, only a huge desk sitting in the open barren desert.

The MP snapped to attention in front of the desk and saluted. "Colonel Chivers, sir, the men you were expecting are here."

"Excellent, Lieutenant." The silver-haired colonel made no attempt to stand and returned the salute as if he was shooing away a pesky fly. "You may return to your post."

"Yes sir," the MP saluted smartly, spun and strode off into the night.

"I would offer you gentlemen a chair, but you will not be staying long," the colonel's voice was smooth and cold as wind coming off a glacier. "There has been a plane crash, but the situation is being dealt with quite efficiently by the military. I'm afraid civilians, no matter how well intentioned, would only be in the way and could hinder our operations."

"Nice desk," Sheriff Sinrod said, making no attempt to mask his anger. "Apparently you were expecting us. Perhaps we should get better acquainted. You're Colonel, ah, Chivers?"

The officer leaned back in his chair and laced his fingers behind his head. "Correct, *Mister* Sinrod. I prefer to be addressed by my full name and rank, which is Colonel Randall Chivers, United States Army Intelligence."

"Okay, *Randy,*" Sam said, relighting his stub of cigar. "I'm Sam Sinrod, the duly elected sheriff of this county and my friend here is Dr. Bryce Whitlock, the coroner of Grant County."

Whitlock spoke up to help defuse what he perceived as a certain confrontation that would be best avoided. "Colonel, sir, you said a plane crashed here."

Colonel Chivers unlaced his fingers and adjusted his sunglasses. "Yes, it was a military cargo plane carrying cleaning solvents that was heading for the Air Corps base in Roswell. A very unfortunate occurrence. Not only did it result in the deaths of the crew, but the exploding chemicals rendered the entire area *quite* hazardous. As you can see, we are sterilizing the zone of contamination."

Sam Sinrod snorted, "This so-called plane crash only happened maybe fifteen minutes ago. You're already here with bulldozers, trucks and probably over a hundred men. We live here yet you were waiting for us to show up. What gives?"

Colonel Chivers sat upright; he was much taller than the men had first thought. "You are *most* fortunate that we were on training exercises here when this terrible accident occurred in your fine county. Even the bulldozers are equipped with airtight cabs and their own oxygen supply. Why, the odds are incalculable that such a well-equipped military unit as ours was here to relieve you of such a potentially deadly situation."

"Those men pointed guns at us." Sam immediately realized how embarrassing that statement likely came across and added, "They're lucky I'm in a good mood."

Colonel Chivers grinned with the same keen smile a bird briefly sees on a cat's face. "Yes, everything here is coming along splendidly. I am *so* glad we have seen fit to work together. Bickering and posturing could only result in an already unfortunate situation becoming *much* worse."

"We're just happy to support our armed forces," Dr. Whitlock said, finally able to light his cigarette without trembling from diabetes. "If there's anything we can do to help, you need only to ask."

Sheriff Sinrod stared at his friend as if he had grown horns.

"An excellent attitude, Doctor," Chivers said coldly. "I appreciate that in a man. I do not believe the good sheriff quite shares your opinion at this time, but I'm certain he will come to eventually see the bigger picture."

Sam Sinrod sighed and turned to watch the bulldozers work. His anger had fled as he began to accept the futility of the situation. "Colonel, I think you are quite busy enough without us bothering you further. Perhaps it would be best if we returned to town."

"An excellent suggestion, Sheriff." The colonel leaned back in his chair once again. "To show my appreciation for your help and consideration, I shall meet with you tomorrow afternoon at fourteen hundred hours sharp. You will be in the coroner's office in the morgue at that time. Then we will discuss how this incident and ah, others might be minimalized for the press."

Sam and the coroner exchanged puzzled glances.

"That's two o'clock in civilian time," Chivers said.

"We know that," Whitlock said. "It was meeting in the morgue that threw us."

"This is wartime, gentlemen. The thick walls and underground location will preclude the use of covert listening devices by hostiles." Colonel Chivers stood. "I expect you men to be punctual."

"Oh, we're good at punctual," Sheriff Sinrod said. He nodded to where Payatt Hae and Chepi sat on the veranda. "The old man who lives here is not under arrest, is he?"

Colonel Chivers kept his sunglasses focused on the sheriff. "Mr. Hae is being kept in protective custody until the area is deemed safe. There have been windows blown out of his home and other moderate damage to his property. I personally will see to it that he receives prompt payment from the military."

Sam Sinrod nodded in appreciation. "Two o'clock, in the morgue." He turned to Dr. Whitlock. "I suppose we should be going."

The coroner's mouth fell open. "He's gone. Just like that!"

Sam saw only an empty chair behind the desk. "Well, I'll be. In all of my born days I've never seen anyone vanish into thin air before."

"I'll escort you gentlemen to your car," Chivers' smooth voice chimed dozens of feet behind their backs, startling them. "It will be, ah, safer if I do."

Dr. Whitlock and the sheriff spun in amazement. The colonel motioned for them to follow him.

"Thank you, Colonel Chivers," Sam said. Both men silently agreed the officer was aptly named as they followed him to their still-running cruiser.

Chapter Forty-Eight

Payatt Hae did not set foot outside of his home until early afternoon of the next day. The many soldiers had loaded their trucks and strange machines earlier and had gone, but he wished to rest and study on the matter before going to survey the damage. He also chided himself for thinking, however briefly, that a clanking bulldozer could have been an evil spirit.

Fortified by cups of steamy hot Hershey's chocolate laced with sugar from their dwindling supply, Payatt grabbed up the headdress of his venerable ancestor and went onto the veranda. The old Apache had beseeched *Usen* to flatten that windmill, yet his heart was saddened when he saw the once green and tree-covered mountainside had been turned into wasteland, devoid of any living thing.

Very little damage had struck his property, but as all land belongs to all inhabitants, his heart felt heavy. Where green pinon and juniper trees once grew was now barren rock covering many, many acres. Such a travesty against The People could only have been done by *Pinda-lik-o-yi.* No god worthy of notice would ever commit such sacrilege.

Surely, *Usen* was still busy in South Pacific, where it never snowed. Otherwise the great god would have smashed nothing more than a pesky windmill and never let the white-eyes destroy an entire mountainside.

Payatt stepped from the veranda onto dry earth. He watched a tiny lizard scurry to safety before he looked up to see a bank of huge, black thunderheads rolling in from the west.

This was a good omen. Perhaps the great *Usen* had not been so busy after all. A good rain would bring grass and flowers to cover the scarred mountain. Almost as if in answer to his thoughts, shadows canvassed across the dry land, a clap of thunder gave the countryside a friendly shake.

Payatt Hae walked farther into the open. White-eyes, he noticed, always fled the rain. But never did an Indian. Such a wonderful thing as rain in the desert is something to be savored, not avoided.

The old Apache carefully placed the powerful headdress of eagle feathers on his head once again. Last night he had been interrupted from a task he had promised a small spirit.

As the first drops of rain fell onto parched earth, Payatt Hae shook a gourd rattle to the heavens and began a *Gahe* for the soul of little Benny Pegler. Around and around he danced and chanted. After a few moments the old Apache could not be seen for the sheets of silvery rain.

Chapter Forty-Nine

Sam Sinrod was fishing for a match to light the fresh cigar he had just mouthed, when a frown crossed his face. Being forced to drive in the rain with all of the windows rolled up tight put a real damper on the joys of smoking. He grabbed the cigar and returned it to his shirt pocket.

To add to his irritation, the rubber windshield wipers on the cruiser had mummified, causing him to squint through narrow streaks as he made his way to the morgue.

The sheriff was still rankled over the way that stuffed shirt, pompous Colonel Chivers had treated them last night. Being patronized always did that to him. He was no idiot; those soldiers had definitely been in the area for days. The Army men they had seen in Archie's lounge last night had simply been off duty.

But why was the Army here in the first place? Sam and the coroner had pondered this question over a long breakfast at Ellie's, only to come up blank. Quite obviously, there had not been a plane crash last night. Could, by some totally inexplicable chain of events, the explosion and activity behind Payatt Hae's ranch be connected to the cases of spontaneous human combustion?

You are reaching here.

Sam had spent the day wondering what the sinister Colonel Chivers wanted to meet with them about. He planned to pump the officer for as much information as he could without concern for stepping on military toes.

Sam sighed. He knew full well that playing politics with Colonel Chivers would be akin to tap dancing on quicksand. Anyway, his questions concerning the Army's involvement could possibly be answered shortly. He could only hope. The reporters from big city newspapers were becoming insistent about talking with him. He needed answers.

Rainwater rolled off the roof of the hospital like a waterfall. Overloaded gutters rumbled as streams of water shot out several feet to flatten and run inches deep down the street. When a storm hits the desert, it is always an event. This storm however, was shaping up to be one old-timers would still be talking about fifty years from now.

Holding his hat down firm, Sam bolted from the cruiser and raced the dozen feet or so to the tin covering over the morgue entrance used as a shelter for the hearse. In spite of his haste, Sam Sinrod felt soaked to the bone. He reminded himself not to say a word of complaint. The way this year had gone every voter in Grant County would take the side of a rain storm over a drenched sheriff.

Dr. Whitlock was in the hallway, sitting on Tina's desk, smoking a cigarette and chatting with his lovely nurse, when Sam came in trailing water onto the gray painted concrete floor.

"We've got us a real frog strangler going on out there," the coroner said. "It's about time we got some rain. Much longer and we'd have to retrain the fish in the Gila River how to swim."

The sheriff's humor was at low ebb tide. He glared at the loudly ticking oak wall clock. "I see it's two o'clock sharp. Anybody seen Colonel Chivers?"

"I would imagine the weather may have him running late." Tina batted her green-tinted eyelids at Sam. "I'll be happy to get you a cup of coffee. I just made a fresh pot."

Tina's sweet demeanor and sparkling good looks had a soothing effect on the sheriff's frayed nerves. He reminded himself he had a date to take the lovely nurse to a moving-picture show this evening. After all he had suffered through of late, that would be a most pleasant diversion.

"I'd love a cup, Tina," Sam said, his voice turning cheerful. "And I am really looking forward to our going out this evening. What would you say to a drink at Archie's after the movie?"

The nurse smiled, stood and glided as if she were an angel floating among the firmaments to a table alongside the wall that held a hot plate and coffeepot. "That sounds delightful," she said with sugary words that played a melody on Sam's heartstrings. "That will give us more time to spend together."

Dr. Whitlock came to his feet. "Sam, I think we should head into my office and go over matters while we're waiting on our punctual Colonel Chivers to grace us with his omnipotence."

"I suppose we should." Sam Sinrod smiled as he took the full cup of coffee from Tina. "We'll have a great time tonight. The movie *Stagecoach* is supposed to be a grand one."

"I'm looking forward to it very much," Tina said. Then, with a show of efficiency, she went to her desk and began typing.

The coroner opened the door to his office and morgue, and the sheriff stepped inside, followed by his friend. Both men froze in their steps when they saw Colonel Chivers sitting behind Dr. Whitlock's desk, rolling a jar in his hands as he studied the contents with great interest.

"You're five minutes late," the colonel grumbled without glancing up. "This means our time together will be even shorter." He carefully sat the jar down and focused his sunglasses on the stunned men. "Send the nurse away, close the door, then sit down. We have a *lot* of ground to cover in short shrift."

Chapter Fifty

After the stunned sheriff had sent a bewildered Tina Ortega upstairs to the hospital to get some forms they did not need, he shut the door closed behind him and took a seat alongside the coroner, facing Colonel Chivers.

"What I want to know is how in the hell did you get in here?" Sam Sinrod asked in honest awe. "This room is chiseled out of solid granite. The only way in is past the nurse."

The colonel adjusted his sunglasses. "I *do* have my ways. That is why I am trusted all the way up to General Eisenhower and President Roosevelt. When I am called on for a task, I *never* fail."

"We are glad to hear that," Dr. Whitlock said. He tapped out a cigarette, offered one to the colonel who reached across the desk and accepted it without moving a muscle in his face. "Then maybe you can fill us in on what *really* went on out there last night."

"I can only tell you so much," Colonel Chivers removed his sunglasses. His eyes were pale violet with anthracite centers. "Otherwise I will have to kill you."

If eyes are windows to the soul, Dr. Whitlock thought. *A close look through those black pupils of his would disclose demons waving back.*

"We're not *that* interested," Sam said quickly.

Colonel Chivers replaced his sunglasses and grinned like a snake at a mouse. "I know much about you two. That is why I agreed to meet and tell you what I can. You're loyal Americans even though you are somewhat, ah, *deficient.*"

"Deficient?" Whitlock repeated. "What do you mean?"

"I am aware both of you did your patriotic best to join the military. Dr. Whitlock, unfortunately suffers from diabetes. Sam Sinrod was likewise rejected as being unfit for military service for having flat feet. The fact that you are loyal citizens does entitle you to some answers, however."

Dr. Whitlock turned to the sheriff. "Flat feet?"

Sinrod was also obviously shocked. "Diabetes?"

"Gentlemen," Colonel Chivers' voice was emphatic. "My time here is limited. May I have your undivided attention?"

"Yes sir," Sam Sinrod and Dr. Whitlock said in unison.

The colonel lit his cigarette. "The situation of last evening had its genesis some weeks ago. An airplane carrying part of a top secret project lost an, ah, cylinder that was fastened beneath a wing due to extreme turbulence. It broke off, fell to earth and exploded near a windmill behind Mr. Hae's ranch."

"Yes," Sam said. "We found a fragment of it."

"This top secret project you mentioned," Dr. Whitlock said, his eyes sparkling with sudden understanding. "It must be an experiment in genetics!"

"Ah," Chivers nodded in satisfaction. "You impress me, Doctor. I will tell you more than I had planned. Our scientists have discovered it is possible to cause a genetic 'incident' using a specific airborne agent."

Dr. Whitlock crushed out his smoke. "This 'agent' was in the cylinder that you lost." He hesitated. "And being exposed to it caused those people to burn up."

"*Excellent,* Doctor," Chivers said. "Perhaps you could be of assistance to us in Los Alamos."

"I'm happy here in Silver City."

"Ah yes, a country doctor at heart," Colonel Chivers blew a

smoke ring to the ceiling. "That fits your profile perfectly."

Sam Sinrod spoke up, "If the stuff that fell off that airplane caused those people to catch fire, why didn't a lot more burn up? A secret weapon that kills only nuns and banjo players doesn't seem terribly useful."

Colonel Chivers gave a sigh of impatience. "Sheriff, you are not grasping the true potential of such a weapon. Imagine Hitler giving a speech and burning up in front of thousands. Then add Mussolini, Hirohito, all of the Axis leaders going up in flames. Panic would reign and we would win this war in no time."

Dr. Whitlock turned to Sam. "DNA is very specific to the individual. A genetic attack would require a sample of the target's DNA, then the 'bomb' would be dangerous only to those people who fit the extremely narrow attack perimeters."

"*Very* good, Doctor," Chivers said. "You have explained why those few unfortunate people caught fire and also why we are experiencing extreme difficulty deploying this agent as a weapon. Obtaining a DNA sample from Hitler is no easy task."

"If you're that close you might as well shoot the bastard," Sam opined.

"Ever the pragmatic," Colonel Chivers said. "Unfortunately, you are also correct. The genetic experiments are not coming along so satisfactorily as are . . . *others.*"

Whitlock lit a fresh Chesterfield. "Then the seven cases of spontaneous human combustion here were strictly random, caused by exposure to a secret genetic agent."

"One that was *accidentally* released," Chivers added quickly. "Once we discovered what had happened, the area was deemed hazardous. As anyone with the specified genetic triggers would be in danger for decades to come, the decision was made to sterilize the area using napalm, which occurred last night. There is nothing further to fear from this unfortunate occurrence. The source has been eliminated and the, ah, substance that was released has, by now, dissipated harmlessly."

Sam Sinrod cocked his head. "And just like that, it's over. Seven innocent people are dead. I can't explain to anyone what happened to them, while you continue on your merry way."

"Ah, Sheriff, you misinterpret my altruism," Colonel Chivers said with a puff on his cigarette.

Dr. Whitlock turned to his obviously puzzled friend. "He's sorry and going to help us out."

Colonel Chivers laughed, and it sounded like ice cubes rolling on steel. "True, if you listen carefully and do not take foolish liberties."

Whitlock and the sheriff nodded in agreement.

Colonel Chivers continued. "What we say is that last night a military cargo plane crashed. This is a small news item considering what is going on in the world. I have considerable influence in your state. If you two men play ball with me, I will see to it that most of the media attention you are receiving simply goes away. The rest will fade in time. Put down those unfortunate people's deaths as due to fire of unknown origin. File them away and go about your business. Nothing more will come of it unless you foolishly provoke me by speaking out."

"All we know about is that plane crash last night," Sam said.

Dr. Whitlock nodded. "Our country is at war. We will do our part."

"Excellent," Colonel Chivers chimed. "I just *know* I can trust you men."

Sheriff Sinrod and Dr. Whitlock watched as the colonel stood and left by the door. Neither could hear a whisper of footsteps.

"What do you make of that," Sam said, obviously still thunderstruck. "A plot to kill Hitler goes astray in our jurisdiction. Who would have dreamed it?"

"It is just too bad seven innocent people had to die because of an accident."

The sheriff tasted his coffee and frowned. "I hate cold coffee." He rolled his eyes to focus on the black widow spider that had taken Benny Pegler's life. It floated serenely in a jar of clear liquid. "I imagine we can trust the colonel's word that what happened here *was* a total accident. And that it *is* all over."

Dr. Whitlock pushed his chair back wordlessly and walked from the morgue. Sam followed. In a moment they both were standing outside under the canopy where Thornton's hearse was parked. Rain fell in thick sheets while drumming on the metal roof.

The men stood side by side, watching the rain for several minutes.

"We'll never know, will we?" Sam said over the rumbling of the rain. "All of this might have simply been a way to test whatever the hell it was they were working on."

Dr. Whitlock surprised him by asking, "Did you ever read Adolf Hitler's book, *Mein Kampf*?"

"No."

"You didn't miss a lot. Hitler's a lousy writer and awfully boring along with being self-centered, but one thing he wrote sticks in my mind: 'No one ever asks the victor if he told the truth.' "

"Yeah," Sam said, heavy in thought. "I suppose Hitler might have been correct at least once. Even a busted clock is right twice a day."

"I'll swing by your place at six-thirty," Dr. Whitlock said, attempting to be cheery. "Then we'll pick up our dates and head for the movie house."

Sam smiled. "We really need a break like this, the company of two beautiful girls and being able to watch people getting killed on their way to Lordsburg. I wouldn't miss it for the world."

Dr. Whitlock watched his friend melt into the life-giving silvery rain. Then he turned and walked slowly back to the morgue.

The answers to some questions are best left to the ages.

ABOUT THE AUTHOR

Born in the shadow of Pike's Peak, **Ken Hodgson** has enjoyed various and interesting careers. He has worked in a state mental hospital, been a gold and uranium miner and prospector and owned an air-compressor business. A former newspaper columnist, Ken has written hundreds of magazine stories and articles along with over a dozen published novels. He is an active member of both Mystery Writers of America and Western Writers of America.

Hodgson resides in San Angelo, Texas, with his wife Rita and totally spoiled cats, Penelope and Ulysses.